HOSEA

THE PROPHET WHO MARRIED THE PROSTITUTE

BY JOSEPH DESCANS

A wholly owned subsidiary of **TBN**

Hosea

Trilogy Christian Publishers A Wholly Owned Subsidiary of Trinity Broadcasting Network

2442 Michelle Drive Tustin, CA 92780

Rights Department, 2442 Michelle Drive, Tustin, CA 92780.

Trilogy Christian Publishing/TBN and colophon are trademarks of Trinity Broadcasting Network.

Cover design by: Trilogy

For information about special discounts for bulk purchases, please contact Trilogy Christian Publishing.

Manufactured in the United States of America

10 9 8 7 6 5 4 3 2 1

Library of Congress Cataloging-in-Publication Data is available.

ISBN: 978-1-68556-675-3

E-ISBN: 978-1-68556-676-0

This book is dedicated to the Holy Spirit, the One who inspired me to write it and helped me all along the way. Thank You, Holy Spirit!

TABLE OF CONTENTS

Chapter 1—The Call.............................7
Chapter 2—The Pick-Up.........................11
Chapter 3—Going for a Drive...................25
Chapter 4—A New Home..........................47
Chapter 5—Debutante...........................65
Chapter 6—Hitched.............................79
Chapter 7—Justice.............................83
Chapter 8—The Café............................87
Chapter 9—Katie...............................95
Chapter 10—Fast Food Prophecy................107
Chapter 11—Baby Grace........................113
Chapter 12—The Little Foxes..................115
Chapter 13—Soap at the Nail Shop.............125
Chapter 14—Wanderlust........................133
Chapter 15—The Wine Debate...................137
Chapter 16—The Grace Debate..................143
Chapter 17—The Flesh Debate..................151
Chapter 18—Where Are Those Papers?...........159
Chapter 19—Foreign Tragedy...................169
Chapter 20—The Jewel.........................173
Chapter 21—The Departure.....................179
Chapter 22—The Party.........................183
Chapter 23—The Homecoming....................189
Chapter 24—The Grocery Store.................193
Chapter 25—Mercy.............................199
Chapter 26—A New Woman.......................205
Chapter 27—The Birthday Surprise.............213
Chapter 28—When Is Mommy Coming Home?........219
Chapter 29—Surprise..........................223

CHAPTER 1—THE CALL

A shroud of subdued surrender enveloped Hosea as he gazed at the telephone on the desk before him. With glazed and bloodshot eyes, he cut the silent stillness by reaching out and picking up the receiver. After many sleepless days of lamentation, he had finally broken down to a place of resolve to initiate the first act, which would change his life forever in a direction that he could only dread, but it would be an act of obedience to God. The son of a fiery minister, who was the son of a minister, the son of a minister for as far back as his family tree could chart, at twenty-seven years old, he stood to break the line of marital purity and consecration that had marked his family for generations. He was just grateful that his parents were not alive to see it; this was his only earthly consolation. He knew God had a plan for him. He knew his father had named him Hosea Daniel for a reason, and now he knew why. (Hosea, MEV)

He punched the buttons on the desk phone, and although his grand house was empty, in a shameful attempt at secrecy, he held the phone tight to his ear instead of using the speakerphone he normally favored. As the numerical chimes turned to ringing, he slumped sideways to lean on his right hand with his elbow on the desk.

"Charles speaking," interrupted the voice on the other end.

Hosea lurched off his arm, and in his best attempt at normalcy, he responded, "Hello, Charlie, it's me, Daniel."

"Daniel!" he shot back excitedly, "Hey, Mr. Selmo has no sign of any cancer in his entire body. Mrs. Selmo went down to the hospital in the morning like you told her at the Sunday night service, and he was already out of the oxygen tent. He let himself out about a half-hour before she arrived and walked out to the nurses' station in a sheet with all kinds of tubes and hoses hanging off him and sent them into total hysteria. She said he had so much energy when she got there it was like he was ready to run a race. They made him do some tests—"

Hosea interrupted, "I-I-I know. I listened to my voicemail earlier and heard all about it."

"This isn't your cell phone; I didn't recognize the number."

"Yes, I'm calling from a home line in my office; I don't share it because you can't call in." He forced himself to change the conversation, "Pastor, I'm calling because I have something very important to tell you."

Listening on the other end, the pastor's eyes widened, and his jaw lowered as he heard Hosea's declaration… "You what?" He fumbled to find the chair behind him and collapsed into it backward with the phone to his ear. Hosea paused on the other end to hear his pastor's response. Gawking in disbelief, Charles failed to respond for a long moment and then continued, "Bu-bu-bu-bu-bu-but...."

Hosea continued, "I wanted to tell you first...." He paused for a response. "I'm going to get her tomorrow, and I wanted you to know before I did anything. I know this is difficult for you, but I need to go now. Goodbye."

Hosea hung up the phone with the press of a button, leaving the bewildered pastor unresponsive on the other end. He returned the receiver to its place and exhaled a huge sigh of relief. He didn't mean to be so disrespectful, but he just needed to finish the call so he could sleep. He left the massive desk and stumbled toward the long couch in the room. He collapsed sideways onto the couch with his head hitting a pillow on the far end. He curled up his arms and legs and quickly fell to sleep.

CHAPTER 2—THE PICK-UP

Hosea peered over the passenger seat across the busy one-way street from behind the steering wheel of his sedan. He wanted to drive his least conspicuous car but still felt out of place in this part of town, and there was a subtle acknowledgment of his presence by the people on the sidewalks, although they all acted as if he wasn't there. He was looking for a woman. He knew her name and knew that he would recognize her when he saw her but didn't know exactly what she looked like. He felt very much out of place and was startled by a knock on the driver's window. The bedraggled figure just inches from his face asked for some money with an open hand pressed to the closed glass. "No," Hosea exerted from behind the glass, shaking his head. The man pounded the glass once with his closed fist and started walking down the sidewalk, glancing back and babbling gibberish, cursing and waving his fist back at the car. The longer Hosea's car stayed there, the more attention it drew from the people on the streets. They felt the affluence and wanted to suck the wealth from its owner, draining it to themselves and into the streets where it would quickly disperse into untold countless directions, never to return, and indiscernible that it ever was.

Hosea returned his gaze to the opposite sidewalk many yards ahead of his car. He recognized the woman he needed to meet standing there. With her thick blonde hair and high heels, she already looked several years beyond the tender age of nineteen. He saw her profile as she spoke with a man sitting on a crate next to the building who spoke back to her roughly as if addressing his own personal, despised possession; he looked at the ground as he spoke to her. She produced some money and held it to his face as she had done for nearly two years. He reached up to take it from her hand and lowered it to his lap to count it. He acted as if there was not enough and began to interrogate her. She defended herself with a few words before his hand shot up like a striking cobra, seizing her wrist. He pulled himself up by her arm and, without another word, walked her out of sight through the apartment door at the top of the steps.

Absorbing the scene, Hosea put his hand to his temple and leaned on the steering wheel. After a moment, he sat up and found a number on his cell phone. He punched the button, and his phone started vibrating.

Sitting at a restaurant table waiting for an appointment to arrive, Pastor Charles eyed the number on his cell phone screen. His posture stiffened, and he paused before answering, "Hello, Daniel?"

"Charlie, it's me again," affirmed Hosea.

"Yes," the pastor answered guardedly.

"Do you have Roy's number offhand? You know, our friend that we meet for golf sometimes," he asked somewhat awkwardly, considering their last conversation.

"The detective?" questioned the pastor.

"Yes, do you have his number on your cell phone?"

"Yes, of course, I do. What has happened, Daniel? Are you in trouble? I'm surprised you called me back; I didn't think I'd hear from you again—"

Daniel interrupted, "No, no, I just need to ask him a favor. I have a little something I could use his help with."

"What's going on there, Daniel? Has this something to do with—"

(Interrupting), "Well, yes, but—"

(Charles interrupted) "Actually, now is not the best time to talk about this, I'm having lunch in a minute, but let me just get you his number from my phone, let me hang up, and I'll send it to you right now."

"Okay, thank you." Daniel hit the button, dropped the phone on his lap, and looked across the street. After a few seconds, the phone chirped to signify the receipt of a text, and he made the next call.

Seated at a desk in his downtown office, Roy glanced at his cell phone when it rang and reached over to pick it up. "Hello, Detective Schwartz here," he spoke with authority.

"Hello Roy, this is Daniel; how are you doing?" he said

cheerfully.

Surprised by hearing Daniel's voice, "Doing well, thank you, what could *you* be calling me for?" the officer asked.

"Well, I think we could do each other a favor. I'm downtown here on Market in front of this restaurant..." He looked for the sign out the window, "Al's Eatery, between 7th and 8th street."

"What are you doing down there?" Roy asked indignantly.

"Well, there's a guy here in an apartment across the street in a slick purple, pinstripe suit with a purple hat, with a feather—"

"Stan?" interrupted Roy, obviously knowing the man he described.

"Well, I don't know his name, but—"

"What are you doing there? That guy is a killer..." he responded excitedly.

"Well, I've been here for a little bit, and I've seen some packages exchanged and different men and women coming and going—"

"Packages?" he interrupted again.

"Yes, he got a big one in a paper grocery bag and went inside, and then there was this influx of people coming and going right after he got the paper bag..."

"So, you're just hanging out watching this pimp sell drugs? What are you doing there? Why are you there?"

Roy returned emphatically.

"Weeeell…" Hosea answered reluctantly, "I thought you might know who this guy is aaaand…"

Looking at a picture on the wall of the said criminal, Roy stood up and moved closer to the tack board, "Yeah, that's Stan the businessman, as he likes to be called, we all know who he is here, and if you've been watching this cut-throat you are in grave danger, you need to leave now!"

"Well, I can't go just now—" he answered naively.

Roy interrupted with increasing intensity, "What do you mean you 'can't leave now'?"

"Uhhh," Hosea stalled, trying to think of how he should answer.

Roy, feeling Hosea's lack of understanding of the gravity of the situation, responded with urgency, "Okay, it sounds like we can get this guy with some evidence on him, so I'm coming down there fast and quiet. I'll be there in less than ten minutes. Do not move, do not draw attention to yourself. You're parked right in front of the diner?"

"Yes."

Roy shook his head in disbelief and barked out an order, "Don't move an inch!" He shoved the phone into his shirt pocket as he waved to some other officers to come with him, "Rick, Miller, come with me." He grabbed his coat and moved toward the door. He barked at another officer talking on his desk phone as he waved him to follow, "Get off the phone right now."

The officer said to the receiver, "I've got to go," and put the phone on the receiver as he rose from his seat. "Yes, sir!"

Hosea looked across the street at a woman in stilettos and a short-skirted bright blue dress and long, full wavy brown hair. The woman stood a couple of doors down from where Stan had entered.

He opened his car door and stepped out with a large manila envelope tucked under his sports jacket. He closed the door and locked it with a *chirp* as he walked across the street toward the woman. She saw him coming as he crossed the street. His fine-pressed suit and shiny black shoes stood out brightly amidst the dinginess of the surrounding ghetto. Her eyes never broke their gaze until he stepped up the curb in front of her. "Hello, ma'am," he said politely while looking her straight in the eye. "Could you please introduce me to Candace?"

"Candace?" she questioned, leaning to the right and putting her hand on her hip. "You mean Candy?" she asked coyly and then pressed him, "What do you want her for?"

Hosea answered in a stately manner, hiding how uncomfortable he actually felt, "I have some business to discuss with her."

"Business, huh?" She looked him over from head to foot again, admiring his stature, fine clothes, and handsome face. He was substantially more attractive and affluent than the regular fare. "What about doing business with me?" she asked candidly.

"Well," he chuckled nervously, "I-I really need to speak with Candace. I mean, Candy."

"Candy, huh...? It has to be Candy," she returned sharply. She narrowed her eyes down to a squint and pursed her lips in an interrogative manner. Despite her hardness, she possessed a captivating beauty. "Well, I'm Donna; you should do business with me next time," she retorted as she turned and headed toward the apartment door. "Wait here," she called back indignantly without turning around.

Hosea folded his hands on his belly and watched her ascend the steps about thirty feet away. As she passed through the door, he looked at a man watching him from the bottom steps nearby and tilted his head as if to say hello. The seated man silently tilted his head to acknowledge Hosea and then turned his eyes away. Hosea looked around for a brief moment before Candace emerged from the door. She walked toward him and stopped where Donna had been standing.

"So, you would like to do business with me?" she asked with piercing blue eyes and vibrant red lips. There was very little attractive about her; the fresh coat of lipstick and bright clothes did little to cover her disheveled appearance and the wear of her lifestyle on her countenance. Her demeanor conveyed the understanding that however handsome this man may be, he would only use her for a brief time and then cast her aside like everyone before him, leaving a small token of his selfish appreciation behind.

However, Hosea didn't see any of this. The first instant that his eyes met hers, he looked deep down into her soul and saw the beauty and intrinsic value of the person God created before He placed her into her mother's womb. In a flash, he saw the eternal purposes of God for her life and beauty very different from what the natural world could see. This vision was indelibly branded on his mind and moderated his every thought toward her from that moment forward; he did not see how she actually looked at that moment, but only what God originally intended her to be.

In light of that vision and the bond it created, her inherent beauty outshined the hardness that years of abuse had etched on her body and character. In his eyes, there were no wrinkles, cuts, scars, or even smudges in her makeup. Hosea paused for a moment, wondering how such a beautiful woman could be in this place.

"Yes," he smiled back at her disarmingly and gestured toward the diner across the street while extending his hand. "Can we talk at Al's for a moment?"

Candace could not fathom what had happened when he looked into her eyes, but she felt it in the most inexplicable and supernatural way. "Talk?" she asked candidly, maintaining composure despite her surprise. "At Al's?" She tilted her head sideways, looking at him curiously.

"Yes, talk…at Al's," he returned smiling.

She stood looking at him for a moment until he warmly

leaned toward her and put his hand on the small of her back to direct her towards the diner, acting as if he were a long-time and endearing gentleman friend. She turned toward the street slightly, and when his fingers touched her spine, a wave of tenderness swept over her, and her hardness gave way to long-forgotten, gentle femininity. Her legs weakened as she stepped off the curb, and, like a car recovering from a backfire, she caught her balance by lurching forward into the street and continued walking.

Hosea quickly looked for traffic and then walked her across to the diner without a word. She was swept by his handsome face, his stature, and fine clothes, and more so by his calm, assuring presence. She struggled to keep her composure, but she couldn't help feeling like a young girl again, like a teen on prom night with her dreamboat, quarterback boyfriend with rich parents. This was strange.

He opened the door to the diner for her, and as she passed through the doorstep, her euphoria subsided as her street mind switched back into gear. She straightened up, scanned the room, and went ahead of him to pick a seat at a table where she could see across the street to Stan's door. She pulled out a chair, and Hosea unexpectedly stepped up behind her to push it in as she sat down. He moved to the other side of the table and sat down facing her. She looked over his shoulder at Al's door, and Daniel's car was visible to her right through the large glass window. He pulled the envelope out of his jacket and put it on the table. He pulled a small stack of papers out and fingered through them until he found the place he wanted to show her. Her eyes pivoted between the papers and the window.

She looked at the papers with perplexity, bewildered by the strange sequence of events and emotions that had occurred over the last few minutes. This isn't what she expected when he said business. Daniel's heart pounded, but there was no sign of it in his countenance or body language. Once he found the place he wanted, he tilted the papers toward him a little and began to speak.

"Candace," she flinched when he said that name. "I have a proposition for you," he said in a calm, friendly, business-like manner.

Puzzled but enamored by his smile, she answered inquisitively, "What is that? And how do you know my name is Candace? I haven't heard that in years."

"Well, I can explain that later, but I would like to…" he cleared his throat as he showed the first sign of discomfort and then recomposed himself, "hmm, well, for you to marry me and mother my child."

"To do *what*?" she burst out.

Daniel recoiled at her outburst but quickly recovered. He turned the papers in her direction and slid them toward her, pointing to the place he wanted her to see, and blurted out earnestly, "Yes, and I'm willing to compensate you for your efforts." Daniel had wrestled terribly about how to make this proposition and had concluded that there was no easy way. He felt as if he were hurling himself bound and gagged onto the railroad tracks of destiny, but at the same time desperately hoped that this beautiful woman would agree that very moment.

Confused and calming slightly, she continued, "My efforts? What are you talking about? Pay me to get married and have a kid?"

"Well, it's actually more of a prenuptial agreement," he stated matter-of-factly with his eyes turning to avoid hers. He focused back on the papers to divert her attention from his awkwardness. "Please look at what I'm willing to do for your commitment."

Amused, flattered, and profoundly confused by the proposition from this stranger but also warmly captivated by the thought of being taken away from this horrid life by this handsome man, her mind spun for a moment, and she asked dazedly, "My commitment?"

"Yes, please look at the paper," he said earnestly with his finger in place.

She gazed at him momentarily in an emotional drunken stupor. She now thought that she was in a drug-induced dream, not the familiar nightmare, but a dream. She hoped it was a dream but feared it might turn back into a nightmare. He continued pointing at the paper, but she couldn't look away from that face. He motioned his eyes toward the paper, and she sobered just enough to follow his eyes down to his finger; she squinted to focus on the numbers. Her eyes widened, and her mouth dropped open. "You're going to pay me that much? For having a baby?"

She was overjoyed but confused and could not believe what was happening. She couldn't imagine having a baby;

it seemed impossible to her. A real prince sat before her wanting to pay her to have his baby! Not just to marry her but to have his baby. Her mind couldn't absorb this concept but having a baby was unfathomable.

"Yes, but if you want, well, I was hoping we could stay married, but if it doesn't work out for you, you will be compensated for having a baby; there is actually a provision for three," he answered sheepishly.

She jerked her head back suddenly, and he jerked back in response. "Three? I can hardly imagine having one! I'm not having more than one!" She raised her hands and looked at the ceiling as if she were addressing God. "What am I saying?" She put her head in her hands in total disbelief and confusion. "What is happening to me?"

"You don't *have* to have three," Hosea backpeddled, extending his hand toward her.

As she sat with her head in her hands, reality suddenly hit her. The inflating balloon of hope popped as she looked up at Daniel and asked in a sarcastic panic, "Do you think Stan is going to just, just going to let me walk away from here? Ride off into the sunset with some cowboy prince charming. He's going to want a cut of this," poking the paper with her finger, "a big cut. He's a businessman. He knows you've been sitting there watching him for the last half-hour; he just hasn't decided what to do about you yet. He's…" She glared out the window with dread. "Uh oh," she continued ominously, "he's coming."

Daniel turned to see Stan stepping off the sidewalk with

a strong, steady gait, looking sternly in their direction. Unflinching, he did not look for traffic but strode vengefully toward the diner in his pinstriped, purple suit. As he passed the center of the street, the guy on the steps behind him jumped up and dashed into the apartment just before a black police car screeched to a stop at the curb. Two seconds later, another police car screeched to a stop a few feet from Daniel's car, blocking Stan's path to the diner. Roy opened the passenger door and jumped out with his gun drawn, and pointed at Stan. "Freeze! Put your hands in the air!" he shouted. The man in purple didn't look away from the diner but stopped and raised his hands as the police car driver grabbed him by the collar and swung him toward the car, pressing his face against the hood and pulling his hands behind his back to cuff him. All of the other people fled the scene.

Daniel and Candace gawked out the window for the next moments as Stan was cuffed and pulled up off the car. He stood there for a moment, looking straight at them with a vengeful glare before they swung him toward the back car door and shoved him into it. Other police cars arrived, screeching to a stop in the street. Candace gasped when an officer emerged from the apartment door with a large paper bag. She knew she was going to need that in a few hours. The guy on the steps came out with his hands cuffed behind his back and a policeman pushing him toward a squad car. Several women, including Donna, also came out of the apartment cuffed, cursing and struggling against the officers as they put them in the cars.

Once the threat of a gunfight subsided, the street began to crowd with people, and more police cars arrived. Eventually, Daniel turned back around toward Candace. She saw her life disappearing before her: her drugs, her pimp, her apartment. Candace and Daniel looked at each other for a moment. Candace with a numb blankness of disbelief and Daniel with a happy expectation of taking this woman home today. "Well," he said, smiling boyishly. "It looks like we are going to be here for a while. Would you like something to eat?"

She looked down at the paper and back up at him, "Yeah, where do I sign?"

CHAPTER 3—GOING FOR A DRIVE

Candace knew Daniel had to have some serious cash because of his clothes, his car, the way he carried himself, and mostly because of the figures on the contract she signed. Seated in the front seat of his sedan, she prodded him with many little questions to find out exactly how much he was worth and how he got it. He cleverly avoided answering these questions, and they enjoyed parrying back and forth over the issue. He didn't want her to know that information yet, and he wanted her to experience the full surprise impact of his mansion when she saw it. They bantered back and forth, laughing and chatting as they left the ghetto where she lived.

They had barely left the city when Daniel slowed and hit a button on his dashboard. A gate began to open on the right-hand side of the road, and Candace looked over to see a three-story mansion and estate which took up an entire city block; she gasped lightly. Hosea turned into the driveway facing a six-car garage and hit another button which opened the far-right garage door. The front gate closed behind them as he passed over the driveway and rolled into the one empty space in the garage.

From her seat, Candace peered past Daniel to get a look at the three other cars. With six doors in the garage, she expected to see five other cars. There was a shiny tan four-wheel-drive Toyota Sequoia fully modified for off-roading next to them, blocking her view of the other cars. She opened her door and stepped out next to the door going into the house. It was a spacious garage with at least six feet in front of their sedan to the wall and at least four feet between the cars. The garage was all white with a red-painted floor. It looked very clean. She had forgotten about Hosea as she stepped forward to see the other cars. He watched her from his seat as she rounded the front of the car toward the other cars. Beyond the Sequoia was a black Lincoln town car; it looked like it had a satellite dish, radar, and some other antennas on it. After the Lincoln was the one she was looking for, a shiny, bright metallic blue Ferrari LaFerrari. She gasped again when she saw it and kept moving without breaking her gaze. Daniel stepped from the car to follow her, watching her glide toward the sports car. When she reached the Ferrari, she put out her hand to touch it gently, and she lightly slid her fingertips along the body as she did a lap around the car. She loved that car.

Daniel had stepped to the front of the Ferrari by the time she had finished her lap, but she hadn't seen him move. She had become so infatuated with the car in those moments as she completed her circuit, and as she reached him back at the front, she almost walked into him, and he startled her. They looked each other in the eyes for a long, tense, romantic moment. Then he asked her, "Would you like to go for a drive?"

Her eyes widened, and she asked him, in full expectation—as if a long-time dream of hers had come true, "Can I drive?"

His eyes widened to match hers; he tilted back his head and then leaned in real close to her and said with subtle sarcasm, "Uh, nooo." Then he lifted his keychain between their noses and pressed a button. The car chirped; he raised his eyebrows and walked around her to the passenger door and opened it for her. He stretched his hand toward the seat and motioned for her to sit in it, and repeated, "Would you like to go for a drive?" She lurched past him toward the open door and quickly hopped into the seat, and once she made contact, she slowed down to caress the seat with her back and her bottom like she might roll her tongue along her teeth while savoring some exotic dark chocolate. As he closed the door behind her, his eyes rolled back as he pondered this woman's obsession with his Ferrari. He walked behind the car to the driver's side. He got in the custom seat, closed the door, and hit a button that opened the garage door behind them. He secured his seatbelt and started the engine.

As the engine came to life and the gentle vibration waves rolled through the car like a purring alpha lion, Candace laughed with exhilaration. "Woooohooo," she let out with every bit of soul and lung she had.

Daniel smiled and looked into the mirrors before rolling

back into the driveway. Candace was tearing up with ecstasy. Daniel looked over and saw her tears and rolled his eyes and wagged his head. Candace was impervious to this, wiping the tears away, and looking straight out the windshield. She started feeling around the inside again, sliding her hands along everything in her reach until she was satisfied that she had touched every part of the interior in range. Daniel continued to amuse himself with her obsession with his car. The front gate opened and closed behind them, and Daniel rolled slowly down the road as if calmly holding the reins of one hundred Kentucky Derby horses making their way to the starting gate.

"Where are we going?" Candace chuckled.

"Well, I know a place not too far from here where we can open her up, but we can do some curves on the way," he said.

Candace chuckled some more. The car and the entire sequence of events overwhelmed and overjoyed her. She wasn't pacing a street, risking her life with some stranger, or staring at a wall in that dirty apartment. She felt like a wealthy princess wife of an international business tycoon. In a day, she had gone from a…well, she couldn't bring herself to think about that now, to a wealthy princess wife of a super-rich international business tycoon. She wanted to go on the yacht next; maybe that evening he would take her on the yacht. She could feel the horses embracing her. She was high, and the deep, gentle, smooth vibration of that purring lion moved her deepest soul most wonderfully. She was brimming with giggles as she asked him, "Are we going on the yacht after this?" with the utmost certainty that he would instantly say, "Yes, that's exactly what we are going to do."

Daniel lowered his brow and squinted at her for a moment. He had thought she had been remarkably cogent until she had gotten into the car. He had never taken a drug or drank any alcohol; he didn't know how *high* felt. He knew she would probably be on drugs when he picked her up, and he thought he was prepared for whatever that would look like, but right now, he was concerned. Something changed when she got into the car. Was she going to flip out on him? She was happy enough now, but that could quickly change. After a moment of contemplation, he announced candidly, "I don't have a yacht."

That response did not vanish the yacht from her imagination at all, but it triggered another thought, and now she asked him straightly, although giggling, "So where did you get your money from?"

He had avoided the question before, but now he was ready to answer her. "Well…" he started slowly. "When I was barely fifteen, I started my first official 'job' washing dishes at a restaurant. I worked for three weeks and on Friday night was about to get my first two-week paycheck. Right, because you work for two weeks, and then it takes another week for them to process everything, and then, you finally get the first paycheck at the end of three weeks."

"Okay, I get it, go on," Candace injected with her slow, dopey voice so he would get to the point.

"But you do get some little tips every night to keep you going; a little bit till payday..." He reminisced as she rolled her hand for him to keep going and answer the question. "So halfway through the night, I'm in there pushing dirty dishes through the machine, and the other guy, Freddie, is pulling them out the other side and doing whatever he does with the clean dishes to put them away depending on what they are."

"So, you get the dirty work, and he gets the clean work," she injected to convey that she understood. Her eyelids fluttered from half-mast as she spoke, still feeling the euphoria of the purring lion that embraced her.

"Because I'm new. I'm the new guy," he agreed.

"Right."

"So, I'm standing there loading a tray of dishes, and I have this vision."

"A vision?" she repeated. Candace straightened up a little bit because she believed he was referring to a hallucination, and she felt like she could relate to him on that.

"Yes, so it's a little bit hard to explain, and you're the first person I've ever told this to, but..." He became animated and childlike as he told the story. "It's like I saw all of this business, and finance stuff, and numbers, and money, and deals, and people, and places, and machines, and buildings, and real estate; but it's not so much even what I saw but what I knew. Suddenly I just knew a bunch of stuff that I never knew before; I never went to school for it or learned it. At that moment, I understood the big picture of how the entire global financial system worked; it was huge, it's like the entire universe was opened up to me, and I was only fifteen...does any of that make sense to you?" he asked, glancing at her briefly. Daniel has born his heart for the first time about this vision that he still doesn't fully understand himself, and he's genuinely wondering if she understands, as if maybe she can help him understand it better. For that moment, he feels like he's fifteen again, and he's reaching out to her for help to understand this experience.

"Yes, you were hallucinating on the job," she affirmed matter-of-factly.

With his history bubble burst, Daniel came back into context and worked through a moment of disillusionment, remembering whom he was sharing with. He started again, "So, then while this vision is happening, suddenly I pop out of it because Freddy is hitting me on the arm." Daniel changed voices to match the new character, "'Stop daydreaming dufus and get back to work, do you want your job?' he says, and I went back to washing dishes."

"Uh-huh," she said as if she understood perfectly while staring straight out the windshield.

Daniel lost most of his enthusiasm because of Candace's mentally detached responses, but he continued nonetheless telling his story, "So now I know all of this business stuff, and I get my check at the end of the night and look into some stuff about buying stock over the weekend. After school on Monday, I cashed my check and spent almost all of it on this stock—"

"What stock?" she interrupted.

"It was a little one you wouldn't know about, and it's gone now, so it doesn't matter," Daniel continued and again changed intonation and posture as he played the different roles. "But my dad gets home after work and asks me about my check because he wants to make sure I do the right thing with the money, and I had totally forgotten he was going to do that, so I told him what I did, and he totally blows a gasket! 'What! I told you we want to save that money toward your first car, and now you've wasted it, blah blah blah…' 'But, Dad, I did start a bank account, and I kept a few dollars in it.' Less than ten," he clarified confidentially, looking briefly at Candace. "…And Dad says, 'Well, I want to see the next paycheck before you do anything with it, do you understand?' 'Yes, sir,' I told him."

"And so, what happened?" Candace asked.

"Well, I did this father/son financial responsibility save-the-money-in-the-bank-for-a-car thing with my dad with the rest of the money I got from my job from that point on. Meanwhile, he has totally written off the first paycheck and is still a little upset about it and makes a couple of little negative innuendos about it." Daniel wagged his head in annoyance at his father's nagging. "And after a couple of months or less, it is completely forgotten." Daniel looked at Candace as she gazed out the window with her silly smile and glassy eyes at half-mast. She was listening, but he had almost become background noise as she daydreamed, looking out the window. He continued, "So, I'm watching this stock for almost a month, and my money quadruples...and then I'm not *feeling* it anymore, and I've been watching these other things, and I sell the first stock and put my money into the second one."

"You sold it? That was dumb; why did you do that?" Candace interrupted without breaking her gaze out the window.

Daniel rolled his eyes and wagged his head, "I'm not sure why I did it; it must have been God because the next day it tanked," he said emphatically and then continued the story. "And within about six to seven weeks, this second stock skyrockets almost twenty times what I put into it...which is totally unheard of...and then I'm not really feeling that one anymore, so I cash out on that second one and buy a third one with all that money—"

"And let me guess, the second one tanked out the next day," Candace surmised.

"Right, kinda, it started petering out over about two weeks, but then the third one does good for almost four months, somewhere between double and triple my money before I feel like it's not happening anymore. So, then I cash out on that one and split my money up into three different investments. One that it had to sit for a year! That was tough, but I put the rest back into the first one, and then this other one I found that felt good."

"So, you invest in the ones that you (putting her quotation fingers in the air) *feel* good about."

Daniel continued, feeling like she had mocked him with her comment, "Well, not just *feel* but *know*. But if I say *know*, you may think, 'How do you know? Based on a set of facts, a bunch of information you found.' But it's not only about facts and information I found, I just look at things, and I know what is going to happen with them in the future. It's part information and part feeling which becomes knowing."

"You're a fortune teller?" she asked honestly.

Daniel, feeling mocked again, "No, not exactly, but you can call it Spirit knowledge. It's just a different Spirit than the fortune teller; it's the Holy Spirit."

"Oh, that's interesting," she replied as if she was not interested at all.

Daniel felt like he was wasting his time by telling her this story, but he had never told it before and was compelled to continue, "So, in less than a year, I made *a lot* of money, and my dad was driving this beater car that we didn't think was going to live another day, but somehow it always did."

"And you bought him a new car," Candace interrupted.

"Well, close; I bought him a slightly used car that looked and smelled brand new. Because my dad was really frugal, and I wanted to surprise him with a new car, I also wanted him to know that I got a good deal on it. I wanted to cover all my bases when I got him this car. He had no idea I had any money at all, all he knew about was this dishwashing job I did a few days a week, and it was all tightly regulated, and we had to discuss every penny I wanted to spend because I was saving for my first car. So, anyway, I bought this car for him in *cash* one day after school, and then I came back the next day with one of my friends who could drive, and we parked it in his parking space before he got home from work. Amazingly, my mom didn't even notice it in the driveway until he got home. So, he comes home, and I'm doing my homework at the kitchen table, and he's wondering whose nice car this is parked in the driveway, and he looks around for a visitor, and there's no sign of a guest, so he asks my mom in the kitchen cooking dinner, 'Whose car is that parked in the driveway?' My mom has no clue what he's talking about and wipes off her hands, and they both head outside to look, and I'm ignoring the whole thing until they come back inside and ask me *as an afterthought* (acting comically indignant) like I wasn't even there the first time, and I had already decided to work the thing as much as possible, so I pretend not to know anything because I'm doing my homework. 'I don't know, Dad, what's going on?' And he says, 'Somebody parked their car in my driveway, and nobody seems to know whose it is. What's going on here?' 'Well, let's go look at it,' I say, getting up from the table.

"So, we go outside, and I walk them through this whole thing. 'Look, it's unlocked,' and I get in the driver's seat behind the wheel and looking around a little, (getting animated) 'Oh, look, I found some keys under the seat.' And they're standing outside like they're afraid to get too close to this *somebody else's* mystery car. So, then I look in the glove box, 'Oh, look, here's the pink slip,' and I look at it so they can't see it, stalling until my dad asks, kind of aggravated, 'Well, whose is it, what does it say?' And I look up at him and say flatly, 'It's got your name on it, Dad,' and hand him the slip. He takes the pink slip, and I had the owner write in the information, so he doesn't recognize my handwriting, 'What?' he says, kind of demanding, and he and Mom squabble over it for almost five minutes while I'm just sitting there in the seat watching until I finally interrupt them with a big grin (Hosea is glowing as if he's there, reliving the moment). 'Dad, I bought you the car.' Then my dad looks at me, bewildered, and back at the paper and back and forth a couple more times until this big grin on my face tells him that I'm telling the truth. But he just can't understand how I could have paid for it. And they are both staring at me with their jaws hanging open, so I say, 'Do you remember that first check I got from the restaurant?' So, it takes a minute to remember it, then he's thinking, *What does that have to do with anything?* Because he never saw it, but he knows what the other checks were, and that car cost a lot more than one paycheck. Finally, he says, 'Yeah,' and they both are just staring at me with this big grin on my face, and," Daniel giggles as he continues, "they have no starting point to even imagine how I got this car with that paycheck. So, then I tell them something close to what I just told you about my investments but not the vision, and it finally starts to sink in after almost ten minutes. Then my dad gets a little bold and asks, 'So, can I drive the car?' And I said, 'Of course, you can.' So, I hopped in the back seat in the middle, and mom got in the other front seat, and away we went. It had a full tank, and we drove around for like an hour. It took that long until he *really* believed it was his car, and once that happened, he didn't want to waste any more gas."

"Wow, that's a great story," Candace giggled.

They were both quiet for a couple of minutes, reflecting on the story, and Daniel was trying unsuccessfully to read her thoughts by her body language while he drove. Her thoughts drifted from the story to the car, to the house, to the yacht, with little glimpses of Daniel in between. She also struggled to keep a little girl out of the mix that kept trying to pop in. After several long minutes of silence, Daniel announced, "Here come the curves." They began ascending a mountain with long winding curves, which occasionally gave way to tighter turns. Candace fully embraced every curve giggling and making other sounds, accentuating each turn. She rested on the short straightaways to catch her breath. The curves were exhilarating for her, and Daniel fed off her excitement, this little drive was for her, and her elation delighted him. He had never had a woman in that car and never imagined an event like this would happen. Occasionally the road dipped down for a short distance, and going down queased her stomach and felt like starting over again because the curves going down felt different than going up, and her laughs and howls changed pitch and intonation to match. When they finally reached the plateau, she was dizzy from the continuous flow of endorphins.

As the excitement of the curves gave way back to the calming, quiet embrace of the purring lion in the flatlands, Candace closed her eyes, melted into her seat, and drifted into a euphoric coma-like state. Daniel looked on curiously, wondering what was happening in that world she had drifted to without him. After a few short minutes, they reached their destination. When they came to the straight-away, Daniel picked an invisible, would-be starting line and stopped there for a moment in the purring race car. When Candace discerned that they had arrived at the main event, like a waking princess, her eyes opened, she perked up in her seat, and her excitement returned. After one long anticipatory moment, she looked at Daniel and asked giddily, "What are we waiting for?"

"Just checking it out," he responded contemplatively. He lowered the windows and started a slow roll down the road. "We need to take a couple of minutes and check things out first, make sure the road is clean, you know, no road kills or broken glass, stuff like that, and just feel it out."

"*Feel* it out," she emphasized, alluding to their earlier conversation.

"Yes," Daniel looked over with a sly grin, "*feel* it out."

The crawl down the road hardly dampened Candace's spirit. She knew what was coming, and any wane in her excitement was indiscernible. She stretched her neck out the open window looking for glass and dead critters. "I didn't know this road even existed," she announced with an elevated voice.

"Yeah, it's a nice place to visit, but I wouldn't want to live here," he responded, referring to the arid, desert-like surroundings. "I wouldn't want anything to happen to my car here either."

"Oh, yeah, that would be terrible," she giggled, "just terrible." Eventually, they reached the end of the straight, and Hosea turned the car around in a single tight turn. He came dead center in the middle of the two-lane highway and stopped with the single yellow lines ending at the center of his car. With the long, straight stretch of road before them dividing the sparsely vegetated white desert sand, Candace, brimming with anticipation, could not contain herself and erupted laughing boisterously; her laughter burst into a jubilant and frightening scream as Hosea launched into the straightway from zero to one hundred forty in a few racing seconds. He had run this road many times, but her scream made his hair stand up, and every nerve in his body vibrated with the sound. The colored lights flashed quickly on the dash as the RPMs leaped and fluctuated with the changing of gears. That stretch of road seemed very short at that speed, with Candace screaming as long and loud as her breath could go, and as their speed started dropping, it was over almost as quickly as it started. They decelerated more as the road went into a gentle curve, and Candace's scream turned into raucous laughter. When they had slowed enough, Hosea made another tight turn around back toward the straightaway. Candace's laughter turned to panting, and she wiped the tears from her cheeks as they approached his designated starting point. He found the place where the curve went into the straightaway, and he came to a stop, but his stop was barely perceptible before he burst into another launch and Candace into another hair-raising scream as they raced back down the empty highway.

Hosea was normally relaxed when he did these drags on his own, at least as much as you can relax at one-hundred-forty miles an hour and more. He typically came here to relax, but because of Candy's screaming, he clenched his fists on the wheel, ground his teeth, and every hair on his body stood up. At first, he fed off her energy, but now, after the mountain and two launches, his energy started to wane. As he made another U-turn, she laughed hysterically, kicking her feet and pounding the dashboard with her hands and gasping for air, coughing, and then laughing again. Hosea had never seen that much excitement for anything, ever. They came to the place for their third launch, and he waited for them both to catch their breath. He shook out his hands and took some deep breaths to relax, puffing his cheeks and blowing through his puckered lips. Candy's hysteria faded to a popcorn laugh resembling Clouseau's mad police commissioner. She might have stopped, but the expectation of the third launch prevented it. Hosea tightened his grip on the wheel for the next launch and was about to go but decided to wait another minute and dropped his hands. The false start sent Candy into another wave of hysteria; she was laughing, crying, and gasping for air. Hosea slowed his breathing, stopped puffing his cheeks, and looked straight ahead out the windshield, breathing deeply.

Candy's laughing calmed a little, but she was bouncing in her seat and hitting Hosea's arm. Eventually, she calmed enough to catch her breath and got down to a hearty pant, and settled into her seat with her mouth hanging open. They both got quiet for a moment, he looked over at her and she at him, then he hit the gas and looked back to the road. They pressed back in their seats, and Candy went into a long, sustained howl as they sped down the desert runway.

When they finished the third run, heading into the curb, Hosea could see a lone car in the distance emerging from the mountain into the flatland. Pointing to the car, he stated over Candy's diminishing laugh, "It looks like the excitement is over for today; two cars make a crowd on this road."

Candace replied, exhausted and panting, "That's okay, I can't take anymore," as she wiped the tears and mascara from her face and smeared it on her skirt. Hosea decelerated down to cruising speed and continued back toward the mountain. The family in the lone car waved at the racecar as they passed a few moments later, and the unseen couple waved back from behind the tinted glass. The sun was dipping down toward the horizon as they reached the mountain, and Hosea turned on his headlights for the descent. Candace imagined herself riding into the sunset with the Lone Ranger.

Candace dropped down into a quiet, subdued glaze, staring out the side window. She sighed little *ooos* and *whoas* as they went back down through the curves. Hosea listened and observed her curiously as he drove. After they reached the bottom of the mountain, entering into suburbia, she unexpectedly summarized their earlier conversation in dreamy, subdued tones, sounding as if she were speaking to herself. "So, you were hallucinating at your first dishwashing job like in a vision, and you learned how to make money in stocks and investments, so you could buy your dad an almost new car because he forgot about your first paycheck. And you could (slightly raising her hands and fingers for quotations) *feel* the right investments, and when to take back your money, and we can't see your yacht today, but we had a great time at the desert raceway until the other car came, right?"

Hosea looked over at her for a moment and agreed, "Yeah, that's pretty good."

She was quiet for another moment and then looked over at him and asked politely, "Can I go visit my friends for a little bit down in the city? I would really like to see my friends before we go home."

Hosea glanced at her and back at the road. "Well, we're pretty close to the house right now, and I don't think we are going to be able to see any more of your friends after what happened today."

"Oh no, I have other friends down there in the neighborhood who would like to see me right now. I know it," she retorted politely. "They're not in the same place, but they're nearby."

Hosea was feeling slightly concerned about her request and how her temperament may change in the coming hour, but he knew he was just a few minutes from home, where people were waiting for them. "We're going to stop, and I'm going to show you the house now, and we can eat some food and get cleaned up, and you can try on some of the clothes I bought you," he said, trying to change the subject by diverting her attention.

"You bought me some clothes?" she percolated, taking his bait.

"Yeah, I had to get you some clothes to come to my house," he replied, capitalizing on her interest.

"What kind of clothes did you buy me?"

"I bought you all kinds of clothes, a whole closet panel full," he continued enthusiastically. "So, we'll see which ones you like, and then we can get what else you might need, and shoes, and coats—"

"And shoes and a mink coat?" she interrupted.

Hosea laughed. He had enough money to buy a mink coat, or a yacht, or whatever else he wanted, but he wasn't that materialistic. He wasn't bound by the greed that ruled so many people. He saw money and possessions as tools to achieve an end; they were not ends in themselves. He did not feel he had to impress anyone with his wealth, nor did he ever try to manipulate people with it. He continued, "I hadn't thought of a *mink* coat, I'm a little more on the practical side, but the stuff I got is nice."

"Well, I have to have a mink coat," she explained matter-of-factly.

"Why do you *have* to have a mink coat?" he inquired.

"Well..." Candace paused to ponder the assumptions brought about by her newfound wealth. Why *did* she *have* to have a *mink* coat? She didn't really know beyond that. She assumed that that's what she thought wealthy women wore. There was an awkward silence until Hosea reached for the button to open his front gate. He waited for a car to pass and then turned left into his driveway. As the gate closed behind them, a garage door opened in front of them, and Daniel eased the car into the slot, and the purring stopped. It felt like the lion had released her, and Candace suddenly realized that the ride was over, her mouth dropped open slightly, and she stared blankly at the white wall in front of her.

Hosea assessed her for a moment. He was tempted to say, "I'm not against the mink coat..." but thought better of it and said, "Hang on, and I'll help you out of your seat." He lifted himself from his seat and went around the front of the car, smiling at her through the windshield as he passed to her side. His smile broke her stare, and she smiled back at him as she prepared for the door to open. He took her hand and lifted her from her seat, and she wanted to exit as gracefully as possible, but when he touched her hand, she melted again. She tried to lift herself from the car, but her knees quivered under her weight, and she fell into him as she came up from the car, and he caught her with his hands and chest. Embarrassed by her awkward emergence from the car, she liked being caught by Daniel but at the same time felt the need to behave in a manner more becoming of wealth. She wasn't used to being treated like a lady either. He held her arms with his hands and slowly moved her away from his body, and steadied her on her feet. She adjusted to standing, and when they both felt secure that she was sturdy and came to a point where they were looking each other in the eye, he said, "Are you hungry?"

"Yes."

"Well then, let's go look at your room. Juanita picked out some clothes you can wear for the evening, you can take a quick shower, and we'll eat some food. After we eat, I will show you the house. How does that sound?"

"That sounds awesome!" she said emphatically, wondering about the house and the food, but mostly about the clothes he had bought for her.

CHAPTER 4—A NEW HOME

Hosea knew it was just a matter of time before Candace started experiencing withdrawal symptoms. He had consulted numerous experts and had prepared the best he could, but never having experienced anyone in withdrawal. There was still the apprehension that comes with facing the unknown and the inherent risk involved. He had planned his day to keep Candace as occupied as possible with exciting things until the inevitable moment arrived when she would start feeling ill. He knew that every addict dreads going into withdrawal and that she would do whatever she could to avoid it. He had easily ended the plea to visit her friends, but he thought there was a chance she might try to run away. He hoped that he could keep her busy enough with his car and house to create enough desire in her to stay and also that she would forget about the impending need for drugs and that the sickness would catch her by surprise. So far, his plan was working, but as the minutes passed, he knew her time was running out.

When he opened the door from the garage, the lights

came on automatically in the next room. He stood on the threshold leading Candace through the door. As she entered the room, she felt like she was entering another dimension. She stepped inside a gymnasium with a basketball court, weight machines, various other sports equipment, and cabinets with even more sporting things inside. It was bright, white, and spotlessly clean. It looked used but well kept. It was not what she expected, she had not known what to expect, but she was expecting something different, something opulent. The enormity of the basketball court alone was overwhelming. Her eyes widened to capture the size of the room.

"This is my gym," announced Hosea, extending his hand toward the far upper corner and swinging it back as if to unveil the entire area. Candace looked up and across, following his gesture, then all around to see everything. "Basketball court, weight room, man toys, and more," he continued as he walked toward a door on the opposite wall.

"Wow," said Candace in amazement as the door closed behind her. She had always wondered what was in those big mansions, and now she knew: basketball courts. *You do need a big house for a basketball court*, she affirmed to herself. Hosea continued walking across the length of the court toward a door on the other side, leading Candace by a couple of yards to keep her moving. She walked and spun around, taking everything in. Hosea walked ahead. He reached the other door, put his hand on the knob, and waited for her to catch up. Gawking in awe, she stumbled toward Hosea until she almost bumped into him near the door. With a few short inches between them, she looked up into his eyes to see what would happen next. He paused for another moment to create suspense before opening the next door. He turned the handle and pushed open the door keeping his eyes on hers until she couldn't help but look into the next room.

The next room resembled a big lounge with a standard eight-foot ceiling and lots of dark leather furniture and coffee tables and vanilla-colored carpet. In the center, it had a large mini-van-sized aquarium filled with many brightly colored tropical fish. Starting at one end of the tank, a spiral staircase twisted up and over it, ascending to the next floor. There was also a grand piano on the left and a fireplace on the wall to the right. After that was a large dining room and kitchen connected to it at the other end through open spaces. Looking to the right of the aquarium toward the kitchen, a slightly plump, smiling, middle-aged Latina woman in an apron waved at them energetically from the closest edge of the tile dining room floor.

"That's Juanita," said Hosea waving back in her direction and smiling. Candace also waved lightly and smiled as Hosea closed the door behind her. This room wasn't as overwhelming as the sports room, and after surveying it for a moment, Candace honed in on the aquarium. When Hosea saw her looking in that direction, he moved toward the staircase. "Let's go up to your room so you can get a shower," Hosea motioned. "I think that

Juanita has some clothes picked out for you to wear for dinner."

"Oh, wow," said Candace looking at the fish but also thinking about what clothes were waiting for her upstairs. Candace perked up again as they ascended the stairs while looking down at the colorful fish circling in the tank. The fish and the spiral stair combination dizzied Candace, so she turned her focus to going up the stairs behind Hosea. She was sobering up, but the euphoria of the discovery of her new house distracted her from the fact that she would soon need another fix.

At the top of the stairs was a wide hallway going north and south with doors lining both sides. Hosea reached the top, turned right, and then went to the first door on his left, which was open. He stopped at the door, turned to face Candace, smiled real big, and motioned with both hands for her to enter. From the hall, she could see a queen-sized rosewood bed with posts and a canopy, and on the bed laid the clothes picked out for her to wear that evening and the shoes placed on the floor. It was a spacious room with plush, cream-colored carpet and a large curtained window on the far wall. She went straight for the clothes and was surprised to see some pants, a shirt, and undergarments, and there were loafers on the floor instead of some elegant, queenly dress and high-heeled shoes. Her disappointment was obvious, but Hosea kept her attention moving. "We just got you some comfortable clothes for the evening since we'll be eating here, and we can look at some of the other things after dinner," he said cheerfully.

"Oh," said Candace trying to hide her disappointment, before looking around for the closet. She found it, but Hosea directed her attention back to the next task on the agenda.

"Here's the bathroom over here," he said as he walked toward a broad, empty counter with a mirror as long as the counter and a sink at one end. To the right was a curtained opening that separated the room from the toilet and shower. He pushed back the curtain with his right hand and motioned with his left, "And here's the shower." She passed by him to see a spacious room tiled from the floor to the ceiling with light, earthy-colored tiles, a glass enclosure straight ahead, and a toilet to the left. Cream-colored towels hung on a wall rack between the toilet and the shower, and there were small matching cream rugs on the floor. She walked to the center of the room in awe and turned back to look at Hosea. He continued, "I'm going to let you take a shower while I check on dinner with Juanita, but I know it's almost ready, so if you could take a quick shower, I'll be waiting outside the door when you're finished. You can just put your dirty clothes in that basket," he concluded, pointing to a basket on his right.

Still overwhelmed with awe and delight, all Candace could say was, "Okay."

Hosea, conscious of keeping Candace moving, left the shower room and pulled the curtain shut behind him. Candace paused for a moment, taking in the elegant bathroom before her eyes locked on the shower; a sense of ownership seized her, and she stepped onto the rug by the glass door, slipped off her dirty clothes, and tossed them toward the basket. When she stepped into the shower, a large round shower head extended from the wall over her head and began pouring out water as she turned the nobs below. This wasn't the little, drizzly showerhead that barely reached her neck in her old apartment. The way the water cascaded from above, covering her whole body as it fell, made her feel like she was standing under a waterfall in some tropical island paradise. The makeup, sweat, and dirt washed down the drain as she rubbed the bar of soap over her body in hot water. With it went the dirty feeling of the city, her dirty job, all of the dirty people she had interacted with, and the dirty emotions she had lived with for so long. She cried as the filth and pain rolled down off her body, collected around her feet, and flowed into the drain, but when it was gone, and the water was clear again, exhilaration took over, and she began to laugh with joy as a new revelation hit her; it was over, her life of shame was over! She laughed and cried with joy with her hands extended up into the falling water. The dirt was gone, and the clean water was washing her even more. She was emersed in *clean*; a clean house, a clean car, a clean man, and a clean shower.

Meanwhile, Hosea had skipped down the stairs to check on dinner. He was filled with joy and expectation about his future but also apprehension about what the next few hours and days held in store. He knew that as the minutes passed, he was drawing closer to the point when Candace would start getting sick. He knew that, before the night was over, she would probably vomit the food that she was about to eat and was a little surprised that she had made it this far. Juanita met him in the kitchen, and she was also excited. He hadn't given her all the details, but she had watched him struggle over the past few weeks, she hadn't made much food for him, and he had been closing himself in his room and his study for many hours at a time. He was normally open and friendly, sharing many things with her. She rarely advised him, but she was always there to listen and let him talk through his business until he came to an answer. He had little social life, and he went to church, but he had no love life and rarely a love interest. She had seen and heard many interesting things under Hosea's roof; however, when he announced that he would be bringing home a woman, and they would be helping her through withdrawals, and he expected to marry her and start a family, she was at first shocked, but then overjoyed. After that news, the house got busy again. Busy preparing for a woman.

Now Candace was here. Her appearance brought a new dimension of excitement to Juanita as she scurried around the kitchen preparing food. Juanita did not doubt that the woman would be coming, despite the unbelievable circumstances, because she knew and believed Hosea, but when they arrived at her dining room, she was still surprised to see her. "She is very beautiful!" said Juanita excitedly. "I will put the appetizers on the table now, and as soon as she eats the first one, I will serve the other food."

"That sounds perfect," said Hosea. "Let's keep things moving until something happens to change it." Juanita nodded in agreement as she picked up a plate in each hand and headed toward the table. *What do you feed a person that is going to throw it up?* she had contemplated heavily while considering what to cook. She didn't want to make something expensive that would be wasted, but Daniel never did anything cheap, and she wanted the new woman to feel as welcome as possible, so she made the best—but not too spicy. *Whatever you think she will want to eat*, she finally settled in her heart.

Daniel paced the kitchen for a couple of minutes, sampling the food with his fingertips, and then went to inspect the table. Everything was as perfect as he expected, but he couldn't help but adjust a chair before heading back to Candace's room. Daniel walked briskly back to the stairs, grabbed the rail, and propelled himself up. He stopped at the door and listened for a moment. He could hear the shower running and couldn't tell if Candace was laughing or crying. He opened the door, tip-toed over to the curtain, and interrupted her giggles, "Hey, Candace, dinner is ready," he called from behind the curtain.

With conditioner in her hair, she looked in his direction and called back, "Okay, I'm almost done." The conditioner felt and smelled so good that she didn't want to rinse it out, but she felt the urgency of Hosea's call and wanted to get out to see him again. The towels were so soft on her body that they reminded her of teddy bears, and she couldn't help but hug them while she dried. She opened the drawers and cabinets in the bathroom quickly to see what makeup was in there and noticed a little note taped on the mirror just above the sink, "Unless a man is born again, he cannot see the kingdom of God—Jesus." *I wonder what that means,* she thought for a moment before gliding to the bed for her clothes. They went on easily, and she moved back to the mirror for a two-minute makeup application and headed to the door.

When she opened it, Hosea was leaning back on the adjacent wall across the hall with a big smile on his face as he absorbed Candace's new, fresh look. "You look ravishing," he said as she appeared before him. He leaned forward and pointed her back toward the stairs by placing his hand on her lower back, "Shall we eat?"

"Of course," she replied happily before stepping ahead of him. She thought her clothes were nice but not ravishing, so she imagined for a moment what clothes he had in the closet that might make her look ravishing. Nevertheless, she took his compliment in stride and went in front of him down the stairs toward the dining room. She looked at the fish as they passed by the tank, and Hosea motioned her toward the table. Juanita was standing near her chair and directed her to sit down while Hosea stepped up to push it in behind her. He seated himself across from her. It was a long rectangular table, and they faced themselves in the narrow part at the end closer to the kitchen. Candace bit into her first appetizer and looked around a little bit as if something was out of sorts, and the three glanced around back and forth at each other awkwardly for a moment until

Candace said, "Aren't we supposed to be at the ends of the table?" The three glanced around at each other again as Daniel and Juanita tried to understand her meaning before she continued, "You know, one of us should be down at that end, and one of us at this end, that's how they do it in the movies."

Daniel and Juanita looked at each other before he broke out laughing, "Yes, yes, we can do that," he said jovially. "Come, Juanita, help me move things around a bit so we can sit at the ends of the table. Candace can sit over here, and I will sit over there." The change eased the tension a bit for Daniel and Juanita as he made a game of it and started moving things around while Juanita moved Candace into the new seat and served the food. All three of them giggled through the process, and once they were officially situated and reseated with food on their plates, Daniel called from his end of the table with a poor attempt at a British accent, "Hello down there, are you enjoying your food?"

Candace called back with her attempt at a British accent, "Why yes, I am, thank you. It's all quite delicious so far. Are you enjoying yours?"

"Why yes, I am. I always enjoy eating here; the food is always delicious. I hired the chef based on her references and found that she quite met all of my expectations," he replied, winking at Juanita.

Candace continued with a loud voice, "Oh, I do agree also, but could you pass me the butter?" Juanita smiled and moved the butter from Daniel's end to Candace.

While Juanita delivered the butter to Candace, Daniel called down to her, "Candace, if you're not using the pepper, could you please send it over here?"

"Of course, dear, I'll send it right over," she agreed. The two continued sending Juanita back and forth between them like a tennis ball at the US Open until Juanita spun off to the kitchen for another dish. Although the food was very delicious, from the very first bite, it was not sitting well in Candace's stomach. She was able to ignore this at first, especially with the folly of volleying Juanita from one end of the table to the other, but as the food accumulated in her stomach, it became increasingly sour. By the time Juanita headed to the kitchen, Candace could no longer tolerate the discomfort and, without a word, placed her fork on the plate, put her elbows on the table and her face in her hands, removing her thoughts from the world around her and focusing entirely on controlling the nausea that had suddenly overtaken her.

Daniel, responding to her abrupt change, asked, "Candace, are you okay?" After a short pause with no response, he dropped his fork and knife and moved quickly to her end of the table and knelt down, looking up toward her face, "Candace, are you okay?" Daniel's voice was loud and echoing in her ear. "Candace?"

Realizing that she had gone too long without heroin, that she had no way to connect with her sources, and that she would have to escape or expose her addiction to Daniel and Juanita, she was overcome with shame and started crying. She cried because she desperately needed her drug and didn't know how to get it, she couldn't tell Daniel, and the thought of going through withdrawal horrified her. She had no answer, and she needed a fix now. *Why did he bring me here?* she thought. *I can't have babies; I'm a heroin addict.* Waves of shame and despair rolled over her like deep water swells, and her crying turned into deep, heaving sobs with every wave. She felt the strength seeping out of her body as she slowly collapsed onto her plate, pressing her arms into the food. She could hear Daniel calling to her from far away, "Candace, Candace, can you hear me? Can I help you?"

Juanita emerged from the kitchen with another plate of food to find Candace blubbering on the table, lying on top of her food, and Daniel on his knees, entreating her to let him help. Juanita put the plate on the table and rushed toward Candace, put her arm across her shoulder, and leaned into her ear, "Candace, what's the matter? What can I do to help you?"

Candace could hear Juanita but couldn't respond. She was overwhelmed with shame, and the smell of the food under her became repulsive, but she couldn't move. A wave of nausea rolled from her stomach up to her throat, and she convulsed slightly. Now she knew she would vomit soon. This thought sent another wave of shame through her heart and her sobbing intensified. She knew she was getting sicker and didn't want to throw up on the table, so with every bit of strength she could muster, she slowly lifted her face from her hands and leaned back from the table until she was sitting back in her chair with her eyes closed and tears streaming down her face and food stuck on her hands and arms. "Can I please go to the bathroom?" she whimpered.

"Yes," said Daniel quickly. "Let me help you up." He took her hand and moved around behind her to help her up while Juanita wiped her tears with a table napkin.

Candace purposed to stand up, but as she started to move, a wave of nausea rolled up from her stomach, and she eased back into the chair until it passed. Her shame had given way to her nausea and her need to get away from the table before she vomited. She took a deep breath and leaned on Daniel's strength to help her rise from her seat. Her legs shuttered, and her body shook as she shifted her weight onto her feet with Daniel's help. She knew if she opened her eyes, it would make her dizzy, so she kept them closed and let Daniel support her as Juanita stepped back.

As they took the first baby steps away from the table, Daniel spoke quietly to Juanita, "Juanita, can you go get Doctor Leafman?"

"Yes, I'll go get him now," she replied and scurried off.

Daniel directed Candace toward the room he had prepared for her, where the doctor was waiting. "Come on, you can do it," he coached Candace as they moved away from the table.

Juanita ran down the hall to where the doctor was waiting, talking on his cell phone. She burst into the room, waving at him to follow, "Doctor, come quickly."

"Hey, I've got to go now," he spoke into the phone and thumbed it off as he rose from his chair to follow Juanita.

"Candace is sick; we need to help her," said Juanita as she hurried down the hall with the doctor close behind.

They reached Candace just a couple of yards from the table, and the doctor grabbed Candace's other arm to support her. She felt the new person take hold of her but didn't dare open her eyes to see who it was. She was especially sensitive to smell at this point, and the doctor's cologne induced a new wave of nausea which stopped her from taking the next step as she struggled to keep from vomiting. She swayed back and forth, and Daniel whispered to Juanita, "Go get a trash can." She nodded vigorously and scurried back into the kitchen. Candace slowly adjusted to the new cologne smell and felt like her stomach had eased back down out of her throat. She was starting to move forward again when Juanita arrived with a trash can and moved to where she could put it under Candace's head. Unfortunately, Juanita had grabbed a can with an empty can of cat food in the bottom. As the can hovered under Candace, the odor rose up to her nose to create the final wave of nausea that induced her vomiting.

A half-hour later, the three had moved Candace into the room where she would spend the next several days suffering withdrawal. It looked like a sterile hospital room without the electronics and monitors, but it had a stainless-steel sink and a toilet, tub, and shower. Daniel gave Dr. Leafman everything he asked for, which was a lot less than he had expected. "Keep it simple," said the doctor. "We just need a lot of the right food to get the junk out; she will need a bed, a sink, a toilet, a shower, a juicer, and a blender, and I'll take care of the rest, and I'll get you a list of food to buy." The doctor, who had recently retired, was another golf partner of Daniel's. He didn't play golf well, but he did like walking the course and talking with other people, so he often golfed with Daniel, and they exchanged information about business and medicine between them, the doctor helped Daniel stay healthy, and Daniel made the doctor rich. The doctor was already wealthy when they met, but Daniel made him rich.

The next few days were like performing an exorcism on a roller coaster; one moment, Candace would be sleeping quietly, and then, without warning, came the hair-raising screams as she woke from another nightmare—panting and sweating, flailing around in her bed. Stan was a common theme in her nightmares, chasing her, beating her, yelling at her, tying or chaining her up. There were other terrible things too, but he was there a lot, she was always looking over her shoulder for him and as soon as she thought he was gone or had forgotten about him, *boom!* He was there. He always had sharp teeth, long fingernails, and crazy eyes. Stan was a personification of almost every evil thing in her dreams. Although Candace was physically sick, her nightmares were the worse part of her withdrawals. She had three days of incessant nightmares. She would wake up from a nightmare and, in a delirious, nauseous state, sip a little juice or a warm tea that the doctor had waiting for her, shed her sweat-drenched clothes, vomit, or use the bathroom and take a bath. In the beginning, she was so out of mind that she hardly noticed the doctor waiting on her near the tub, but going into the fourth day, she became conscious of the doctor guarding her and started taking showers so he wouldn't watch. When she showered, he wasn't afraid of her slipping under the tub water and drowning. While Candace bathed, Juanita changed the sheets and blankets on her bed and disappeared before the bath was over.

Daniel stayed out of the room for that first week. He didn't want to see Candace like that. He met the doctor outside of the room several times a day but didn't want to see her until the withdrawals were over and she could dress and put on makeup, and they could enjoy a meal together. Juanita was always making juices and teas for Dr. Leafman and Candace. At first, Candace would mostly throw it up, but after a few days, she was able to hold them down, and then she was able to eat more and more. Going into the fourth day, she started becoming more coherent and hungrier. The doctor bumped her up progressively to oatmeal and rice, and then beef and chicken, and then vegetables and bread.

After seven days, the doctor took a break for a few hours and played a game of golf to get some fresh air and exercise. He had spent a week alternating between sleeping on a chair and a couch in Candace's room, waking to shrieks in the night and day. After seven days indoors, he imagined himself a POW as he first emerged from the rich man's mansion-prison into the sunny open air. A few hours of fresh air cleaned out his lungs and his mind before he headed back to Daniel's. Dr. Leafman's wife had passed away about two years earlier, and he had no pets, so there was no need for him to return home. He had already purposed to make Daniel's house his home for about a month, so back he went. He was through the toughest part of the withdrawals, and now he was planning his next phase for Candace, which was a total body cleanse and detox and building a strong, healthy body for having kids. He had almost ninety days to do it.

CHAPTER 5—DEBUTANTE

Daniel knew that before Candace married him, she needed to quickly learn how to conduct herself in a manner consistent with her new status. So, in the days preceding their marriage, Juanita taught her everything she knew about Daniel, his loves, his hates, his preferences in food, in people, in behavior, in life. She taught her about diplomacy, discernment, and feminine discretion. Not just by society's standard but by Daniel's.

As soon as Candace emerged from the detox room with enough stomach and energy to function, Juanita put her to work helping her in the house. Candace shadowed Juanita throughout the day in everything she did; cooking, cleaning, planning meals, making beds, doing laundry, and every other thing great and small throughout the house and property. As they worked, Juanita mentored Candace. One of the first lessons Candace remembered came as they worked in the kitchen, "You must always tell the truth because Daniel already knows everything before he asks," Candace's new mentor advised her. "If you ever think about lying about something because you think you might be in trouble, don't do it! Daniel doesn't care about breaking things or messing things up. None of that is a problem; he just wants to know the truth. If you tell him the truth, he can work everything out from that. No matter how stupid of a thing you do, no matter how big of a mistake, he always finds a way to fix it. He just wants the truth."

At first, this was a tough concept for Candace, who had learned how to say and do whatever it took to get her way and to manipulate people and situations to her advantage. She always tried to read people's motives and agendas before she made any move. Telling the truth in all circumstances, regardless of the perceived outcome or how she could get it to work to her advantage, was a challenge. In the days that followed, she often found herself opening her mouth to talk, stopping herself to rethink her answer, and starting over. After about a week, she realized there was no reason to lie or manipulate anything because no one here would take advantage of her; Daniel and Juanita were always dedicated to her success and well-being in every way. It felt very good settling into this new paradigm of trust. She had never known the peace of not having to second-guess every motive of every person she came in contact with.

Learning etiquette, diplomacy, and personal discretion was a big job for Candace. She wasn't an external processor, but she did say what she meant and didn't mince words. She took a very direct path to whatever she wanted, and she constantly caught herself in her old thinking patterns, and she would stop herself and ask, *How should an heiress act in this situation, or how would a princess or a queen act?* Her image of a princess was the product of the news and the gossip she had often seen about the British royalty, which fascinates so many Americans. She would also reminisce about her childhood memories of playing princess with her dolls. Those fond memories helped distract her from the inadequacy she felt in some situations but didn't always help her learn the proper response.

In Daniel's house, they never directly mentioned Candace's past, ever. They treated her with the utmost respect and honor from the first day. As far as they were concerned, she was a long-time friend who had recently returned to the scene as Daniel's fiancé. She almost felt like a visiting dignitary from a close, friendly country. Juanita chose her words carefully when referring to Candace's recent past. "If anyone ever asks where you came from or where you grew up, just tell them," Juanita counseled. "If they ask about how you met Daniel or about your last few years, tell them you bumped into him downtown, and it was love at first sight for both of you. That will move things in the right direction," she assured. "People usually know when to stop asking personal questions, but if they keep asking, just remember something you like about Daniel or something happy from your childhood and talk about that."

Juanita told Candace that Daniel never got upset, he never raised his voice, and he treated every person, no matter how rude or obnoxious, with dignity. "He never treats anyone different than how he would want to be treated," she affirmed as they folded towels in the laundry room one day. "He lives by that. I have never heard him yell at anyone, even one time, on the phone, never. If he starts getting upset about something, he stops talking. He gets very quiet, and he thinks about the best way to deal with something without hurting people or defending himself before he says or does anything. Every word counts to him, so he's very thoughtful and purposeful with his words."

"Hurting people?" she asked, thinking about Daniel physically abusing someone.

"Hurting their feelings or their reputation, belittling them in any way," Juanita clarified. "Dishonoring or disrespecting them."

For two months, Candace never left the property. It was a total immersion crash course in Daniel and Daniel's world. Juanita taught her everything she could think of about Daniel; his businesses, his house, his cars, when he did this, and why he did that. Daniel wanted Candace to know as much as she could about him and his world as possible before they got married and before anyone discovered her there. When they introduced Daniel's "surprise" to the world, they wanted her to be prepared.

Not only was Juanita a wealth of knowledge about everything Daniel, but she was also a very happy person. Every day, Juanita sang or hummed some happy song. She even whistled on occasions. Candace remembered being in that nauseous, semi-conscious state during her detox and hearing Juanita singing some joyful song as she approached her room from the hall, and then she would get quiet before she opened the door. A happy sound always preceded her unless she was talking or listening to someone. Now, every morning Candace would hear the same happy sound as she woke up. She never set an alarm in the morning but often woke up to Juanita's singing.

In less than a month, Candace had all but forgotten about her former life. She no longer felt or remembered the despair and desperation that used to keep her in bed late into the morning and afternoon. Instead, she felt an eagerness to rise early in anticipation of some new joy she would experience that day; the joy of learning something new in her new life; the joy of learning how to cook new food, set the table, or fold some piece of clothing and put it away in its proper place. Everything little thing now was a joy. As she lay in bed one morning, looking up at the ceiling, contemplating her new life, what she might do that day, and pondering her new disposition; her mood, her feelings, her contentment, she came to realize that she was genuinely happy, and she began to wonder why. As she traced the source of her new happiness, she discovered that it came primarily from Juanita. Yes, she lived in a mansion, she was engaged to a handsome, wealthy businessman (although this still didn't seem real to her yet), she slept in a warm bed with fine sheets and a soft pillow, she ate tasty, healthy food every day. The list of all the good things that she now experienced daily went on and on, but her reason for being happy always came back to Juanita. Juanita and her happy songs. But why wasn't it Daniel? She began to contemplate Daniel; how did Daniel make her feel? Daniel was calm and peaceful; he was warm and friendly, he made her feel wanted and desired, and he exuded a quiet confidence in everything he did. She knew there must be some very stressful situations in his international business investments, but she never heard about it and never felt any sense of stress or tension coming from him. At the same time, she never got to see him alone; Juanita was always there. "I don't trust myself to be alone with you," he told her once with a mildly nervous laugh. This only served to stir her desire for him more, but she didn't like the feeling of being kept at arm's length. "We're building a relationship," he assured her with that same friendly, disarming manner he always had when answering her difficult and pointed questions. As Candace lay in bed one morning, a deep grumbling in her stomach interrupted her musings, breakfast didn't take as long as dinner to prepare, but she didn't know what cooking lesson Juanita might have planned and how long it might take, so she decided she should get up before she got too hungry. As she dressed for another day at the house, she could faintly hear Juanita singing somewhere and decided to ask her a question. A few minutes later, she caught up with Juanita.

"Well, good morning, sleepyhead," Juanita cheerfully addressed Candace as she came into the kitchen. "You're getting up late today; I was starting breakfast without

70

you," she chided as she put a frying pan on the stove and turned on the burner.

Candace leaned back on the counter next to the stove. "Well, I wasn't sleeping; I was thinking," she responded, prepping Juanita for her question.

"Really, what were you thinking about?" asked Juanita.

"I was wondering why you're always so happy. You're always singing; you're just happy," she said, gesturing with her open palms lifted in the air and shrugging her shoulders. "I was lying there in bed thinking about why I was so happy here." She paused for a moment before elaborating, "And *everything* is so nice, but it's not because of all the nice things and the big house, but I realized that it's because you're so happy," she said, looking her in the eyes.

Juanita blushed and turned away toward the refrigerator before responding. "Why, thank you for saying that, Candace; that's very nice of you to say that about me," she answered as she pulled out a carton of eggs and a butter dish and pushed the door closed with her elbow. "I wasn't always happy," she reminisced matter-of-factly as she moved back toward the stove and put the food on the counter, looking Candace in the face. "That's funny that you should say that because you just reminded me of when my life wasn't so good, and I got to thinking about how unhappy I was, and I was trying to figure out how I could make myself happy." She tilted her head and pressed her forefinger on her cheek like a thinker. "I was thinking about things, and money, and a handsome man that I imagined," she paused, remembering the moment. "And then I thought about another woman in my neighborhood."

"Another woman in your neighborhood?" Candace asked, urging her to continue.

"Yeah," continued Juanita, breaking off a chunk of butter with a spatula and scraping it off into the pan. "She was happy too. I was thinking about how I could get out of that dirty neighborhood and find happiness somewhere nicer when I realized that that woman lived in the same dirty neighborhood as me, but she was always happy, and I wasn't. I don't think she sang as much as I do now, but I did see her singing sometimes." Juanita stopped talking for a moment to break a couple of eggs into the frying pan and toss the shells into the trash. "And that is funny," she said enthusiastically, "because, at *that* moment, I decided to ask that woman *that* exact same question, and I could not rest until I found her."

"Really?" asked Candace surprised at the coincidence.

"Really," affirmed Juanita, motioning Candace to move a little bit so she could put some bread in the toaster. "Her name was Lois, and I found her just before dinner time that afternoon. And I caught up to her, and I asked her…" she stopped again to put salt and pepper on the frying eggs, trying to remember the exact words. "I asked her," she repeated while flipping the eggs one at a time. "I asked her," she repeated a third time while squinching her face as if straining to think harder. "Well, I forgot what I asked her about being happy, but I remember what she said, '*Jesus!*'" she blurted out loudly, startling Candace. "Yeah, she scared me too when she said it. 'Jesus is the reason I'm happy,' she said with a big smile. 'Why do you ask?' Like she was inviting me to talk some more. So, I kept talking and asking her all my questions, and she kept coming back to the same thing, 'Jesus lives in my heart,' she kept saying. At first, I had no idea what that meant, I had seen and heard some Christian religion stuff, and the Catholics fought with the Protestants, and the Protestants fought with the Catholics, and *everybody* I knew used God and Jesus to cuss at each other. None of them seemed very happy except this lady. So, after she said that a few times, I started asking myself, *What does that mean?* and I felt kind of stupid like I was supposed to know already, but then, after she said it a few more times, I finally asked her, 'What does *Jesus lives in my heart* mean?' That made her *really* happy," said Juanita smiling broadly while widening her eyes and bobbing her head up and down in affirmation. "She was waiting for that." Juanita scooped up the cooked eggs one at a time and put them on a plate she had in her hand. "Do you want these?" she asked Candace just before the toaster sprung.

"Yes, I'd like those," responded Candace eagerly.

"Okay, well, sit yourself down, and I'll get your toast. Just butter?" Juanita asked as if she already knew the answer.

"Yes, please, just butter," she said, seating herself on a stool at the kitchen bar and grabbing the fork there.

Juanita quickly spread some soft butter on the toast

before putting it on the plate and setting it in front of Candace with a smile. "Here you go."

"Thank you," said Candace salivating. "What happened next?"

"Well," said Juanita as she slid back to the stove and broke two more eggs into the pan. "She said (taking on Lois' voice), 'I started out a sinner like everybody else, and somebody told me about Jesus and that He could take my sins away. At that time, I was feeling a lot of guilt about some stuff I had done, and I wanted to get rid of that, and I did not know how. I could not see how Jesus could take my guilt away; it made no sense to me. He was nowhere in sight, and I had some very real consequences facing me, but I was just like a dumb sheep. The girl told me more of her story, and then she said, *Take my hand and repeat after me.* I felt blank—empty—as I started that prayer. Somehow, I don't know why I did this, but I consciously emptied myself of all feelings and emotions and even expectations. I had no idea what I was doing or what might happen; I just repeated those words she told me, and when I was done, I felt better. It didn't make any sense to me, but the guilt went away, and I felt good. The next morning when I woke up, I felt different; I didn't feel the pressure, the weight of the world on me, and I was so happy I just started singing…and I've been singing ever since.'"

Juanita took on her normal voice for a moment. "I could see she was always happy, and I didn't see how that could be, so I asked her, 'Don't you ever get sad or angry?' She said (mimicking Lois), 'Yes, I do.' And I asked, 'So what do you do then?' (mimicking Lois) 'I sing louder, (Juanita paused) I sing louder, I sing harder, I sing deliberately at whatever makes me unhappy until I get happy again, and then, when I feel better, I just keep right on singing.'"

Candace was captivated by the story as she consumed her eggs and toast, taking her eyes away only briefly to collect eggs with her fork or to find her toast. Juanita scooped her eggs out of the pan onto her plate, buttered her toast, pulled out a stool next to Candace, and sat down.

"That's what she told me," Juanita said in her own voice.

"So, what happened next?" Candace prodded.

"I said, 'Can I have that? Can I say that prayer?' And she said (in a humorous mimic), 'Yes, you can. You just have to believe in your heart and confess with your mouth that Jesus is Lord and that God raised Him from the dead and you can be saved.'" (Romans 10:9–10.)

Candace laughed at the exaggerated imitation.

"And I said, 'Can I do that right now?' And she said (continuing to mimic), 'Yes, you can. Just repeat after me.'" Candace giggled at the imitation again. "So, she said a salvation prayer, and I repeated every word right after her, and when I finished, I felt better, I felt a lot better, I think I felt even better than Lois. I was so happy I started to cry while I was laughing; it was the craziest feeling. Lois could see that God had touched me, and she hugged me and started laughing and crying with me. I'm sure we looked silly there, laughing and crying, swaying back and forth almost like we were drunk. That went on for about five minutes, and we let go of each other and wiped our tears, and I took some deep breaths, and it was like I was exhaling all my burdens, and I felt lighter and lighter, like I was about to lift off like a balloon."

"I felt like that before," interrupted Candace excitedly. "The first day when I was here in the shower, it felt like all the dirt in my life was washing away. It wasn't as much as what you did, but I felt a lot better."

"I'm sure you did," Juanita agreed. "This is a holy house because we don't let any evil things come in here. When evil things try to come in, we kick 'em out at the door; they can't stand it here in this house," she declared emphatically.

"But I don't think I'm done yet," said Candace with a yearning in her voice. "I never prayed that prayer."

"Well, we can fix that right now," said Juanita, dropping her fork to reach for Candace's hands. "Here, give me your hands; let's pray right now. You can repeat after me; it's easy."

Candace put down her fork and turned to take Juanita's hands.

Juanita grabbed Candace's hands, and they faced each other knee to knee. "Now, close your eyes and repeat after me," she said while she closed her eyes and bowed her head. "Dear Lord Jesus."

Candace closed her eyes and followed Juanita's lead,

"Dear Lord Jesus."

"I am a wretched sinner," continued Juanita.

Candace was repulsed by the word *wretched* but continued anyway, "I am a wretched sinner." As the words fell from her mouth, a deep wave of guilt and remorse swept over her.

"You died on a bloody cross to take away my sins."

"You died on a bloody cross to take away my sins." As she said those words, a stream of horrifying memories of countless sins she had committed starting from her early childhood raced through her mind. She gasped as the thoughts took her breath away. Overcome with guilt and shame, she began to tremble while Juanita continued.

"Please forgive my sins."

"P-P-P-Please forgive my sins," she wailed as she collapsed onto Juanita's lap, sobbing uncontrollably. Juanita let go of her hands and embraced her as she leaned over on top of her. After a few minutes, Candace moaned, "I thought I was going to laugh," and continued crying.

At that moment, Daniel was in his office, immersed in analyzing a building project in Europe. He lifted his head and looked around the room as if he had heard or felt something but didn't know what it was. He took note of the clock; it was almost 10 a.m. He thought for a moment that maybe he had forgotten an appointment, so he looked at his calendar to make sure he hadn't. He thought again for a moment, looked around the room, shook his head, and went back to work.

Daniel had "in days," when he worked from home, and "out days," when he had appointments away from the house. Juanita knew not to bother him until after 5 p.m. when he was home working. Sometimes he would get up early and sit at his desk for eight or ten hours straight. In his home office, he had a full bathroom and shower, a small refrigerator, and snacks. When he needed to finish something, he would turn off his phones or talk on them ceaselessly and work tirelessly until it was done, sometimes forgetting to eat. So, he appreciated it when Juanita broke into his work at five o'clock to feed him and remind him to exercise. When a knock came on his door that afternoon, he knew it was time for his five o'clock break; he was hungry and instantly thought about enjoying his meal with Candace. He rose from his chair and stretched and contorted a moment before heading to the door. He opened the door to Juanita's familiar smiling face, and she said coyly, "That was the longest salvation prayer that I ever prayed."

He snapped his head forward in surprise and joy, but as if he couldn't believe what she implied, he asked, "You what?"

CHAPTER 6—HITCHED

Ninety days passed quickly, and by the time their wedding day arrived, the two could hardly contain themselves. Daniel was very diligent in keeping Juanita between them and never leaving them alone together in the house, but the temptation of having Candace there in the house with him was terrible. Dr. Leafman did a great job doctoring her back to health. By the thirty-day mark, she was looking good; after that, she looked better every day. She was lifting weights, jogging around the property, and even doing some one-on-one basketball with Daniel. Basketball became the most fun, most intimate thing they did. It was a good thing Juanita was always there watching; otherwise, they would not have been able to stop themselves with all that exciting one-on-one touching and bumping. When things started getting too friendly for her comfort, Juanita would call a foul to break them up. Juanita knew nothing about basketball or its rules, so the only fouls she called came when she could see the hormones leading the couple too close for her comfort. The healthier Candace got, the more she radiated with beauty, and the harder it was for Daniel to resist her. They really looked forward to the basketball games, and the last game they played ended quite abruptly as Juanita saw the touching getting beyond the reasonable boundaries acceptable for defense and offense; Daniel was reaching around with both hands, trying to get the ball from Candace—the whistle blew, Juanita broke them up, separated them, pushed them off in opposite directions and they headed off to the showers like wounded puppies. That was the last game Juanita allowed before they married. That was at the two-and-a-half-month mark, just two weeks before their wedding—no more basketball!

When the wedding day came, Daniel and Candace were both more than ready. Daniel spent his last night at Dr. Leafman's house, and early the next morning, the Daniel house was bustling with excitement and activity, getting Candace ready for their wedding. On top of preparing Candace, the couple had decided to have the ceremony and dinner on the front lawn, so by 10 a.m., the florists, caterers, and party preparation people were all coming and going, bustling about, taking direction from Juanita. This was the busiest day of Juanita's life, orchestrating the wedding preparations and getting Candace ready.

When it came time to plan the wedding, Candace was still shy about contacting her family. Daniel was sensitive to her wishes, and it didn't take much time before they decided on having a few people, some simple decorations, and a gourmet dinner. So, in the end, they had Juanita and her husband, Carlos, the groundskeeper, Dr. Leafman, and Pastor Charles and his wife. There was a beautifully flowered arch and a podium, a few chairs set up in front of it, a string quartet set up a few yards away, a large dining table set up on the lawn about ten yards behind the chairs, and that was about it; small but exquisite.

When the time came, the wedding march was played. Dr. Leafman made the long walk from the front door to the podium with the radiantly beautiful bride; he stood her before the waiting groom in front of the arch, podium, and Pastor Charles and sat down. The couple exchanged vows and rings and kissed while two photographers and two videographers dashed about to acquire the best possible recording of the event. The wedding party ate their food, and the couple playfully and respectfully shared their cake with each other before dashing off to the empty house for the night, leaving the wedding vendors to share the remaining food before they left.

The next morning, they were off to a honeymoon island.

CHAPTER 7—JUSTICE

After three weeks in a South Pacific tropical paradise, Candace came back from her honeymoon pregnant. Everyone expected that would happen because everything Daniel did prospered: he married a woman to start a family, so naturally, babies should come soon. There was always a feeling of divine destiny for everything he did. He already had a name for his first son. A few days into their honeymoon, as soon as Candace suspected she was pregnant, she told him so, and as they sat under an umbrella in their modest designer swim apparel on a private beach under the South Pacific sun, Hosea responded happily with, "Yeah, it's a boy. His name is Justice."

Candace was still adjusting to the whole prophet thing, and his response was way too cool for such big news, so she just looked at him in wonder for a moment while she thought, *How does he know that? I wonder if he's right? When did he know that?* She thought she should have been involved in the naming process since it was her baby too. She hadn't paid much attention to the contract she signed, and the fact of its existence was completely removed from her daily thinking. What little she read that first day was almost completely forgotten. She really had no idea what it was for except that wealthy people have such things to protect their wealth. She had a little subconscious notion that it probably stated that he retained all rights to any children they had together, which included naming them. Anyway, she felt a little slighted but quickly adjusted because her adoration of Daniel ran too deep to carry any offense for more than a moment. She finally asked, "How did you decide on Justice?"

"His name is Justice because he's going to revive a standard of justice in the nation," he stated matter-of-factly. "Seeing the direction things are going, it's going to be a tough job, so he's going to have to be, well, tough. I think he can handle it, just like all the other reformers that have come before him."

Candace, still a little confused by his foreknowledge, quietly absorbed and pondered the new information while sipping on pineapple juice from a coconut shell. She quickly accepted the info as fact and started planning for a boy.

After a moment of contemplation, Daniel continued, "I can't wait to see what the little guy looks like; genetics are so fascinating to me. I hope he looks like you." Her heart leaped at that statement, and, impulsively, she reached out and gently, but firmly, tugged on his arm as if to pull him closer. He looked over at her, and she tilted her head to give him a sultry look over the top of her sunglasses. "Okay, babe," he said, acknowledging her intentions. "We'll take a break from the beach in a few minutes." He really needed a break from the bungalow, but he wasn't going to say that. "But really, I hope they *all* look like you."

"They all?" she bantered with an element of shock. "I'm not having triplets! What do you mean *they all*?"

Daniel knew he had slipped his tongue. He thought to stay quiet and hope it would pass, but then, he let go of a long silly "Uuuhhhhh" to ease the tension.

That was enough for Candace. She rose from her seat and stood between their chairs with that happy-determined-mischievous-lusty look on her face, reached down, and gently grabbed his collar with her light, flowery sun blouse hanging over him. Her gentle tugging implied that she requested his voluntary cooperation to rise from his seat. He briefly feigned resistance before lunging forward to boost her tug and rose from his chair. They did a quick kiss, placed an arm around each other's waist, and swerved a little along the path as they headed back toward their private beach hut.

Justice came about nine months later, as expected. Her water broke in the night. Daniel quickly made a couple of phone calls, moved to the car with the prepared bags, and arrived at the hospital about twenty minutes later. Dr. Leafman arrived a minute before them and was barely able to put on his mask and gloves before she started pushing right there at the emergency entrance. They barely got her through the second door, and she gave birth in the emergency room hallway. Justice had come into the world.

CHAPTER 8—THE CAFÉ

The hostess seated Hosea and Candace at a table in the outside court, placed the menus on the table in front of them, and promised to send their waitress in a moment. After a brief overview of the menu, Hosea glanced at a woman seated at another table about twenty feet from his. She was seated with a friend drinking coffee smiling and conversing jovially as the waiter appeared, left them a bill, and took their empty plates. Hosea continued looking back and forth between the woman and the menu with increasing interest toward the woman while Candace placed the stroller with sleeping Justice near their table. The woman and her friend reviewed the bill, pulled some cash from their purses and placed it on the tray, and put a pepper shaker on top to hold it in place.

The woman's friend stood up and excused herself to visit the ladies' room, placed her napkin on the table, and walked away with her purse. Watching the woman's friend leave, Hosea placed his menu on the table and quipped at Candace without looking at her, "Please excuse me a moment; I'll be right back." Interrupted from the menu,

Candace looked up as he slipped away from the table.

"What? Okay," she said, a little confused, her gaze leaving the menu and following him to the other table.

Hosea's eyes were fixed on the unknown woman as he went straight to the other table, weaving slightly around a vacant table between them. He introduced himself briefly and put out his hand. Candace watched as the woman reluctantly offered a limp right hand to Hosea. He asked to sit down in an empty chair, and she awkwardly obliged the stranger to share her table.

From her seat, Candace could see the back of Hosea's head and right ear and most of the unknown woman's face as he continued to speak to her. The woman furled her brows in confusion as he began talking.

A waitress suddenly appeared between Candace and her view of the other table, and she looked up at the cheerful, smiling face. "Hello, I'm Camille, and I'll be serving you this morning. Would you like something to drink while you look at the menu?"

Candace enthusiastically returned the cheerful smile, "Yes, I would like a regular coffee, and Daniel would like an English breakfast tea."

"Daniel?" the waitress inquired.

"Oh yes, he's at that other table." Candace pointed, and the waitress turned to look briefly and then back at her. "He'll be back in just a minute."

"Okay then, I'll be right back. Did you have any questions about the menu?"

"Um, no, not yet."

"If you do, I'll be happy to answer them. Everything is delicious; people love our apple bread. I'll be right back with your drinks."

"Thank you."

As the waitress left the table, Candace's attention turned back to Hosea and the woman. The woman's expression had changed from puzzled to intrigue as she sat quietly listening to Hosea. Candace's enthusiasm for the morning outing also turned to intrigue as she watched Hosea speak to the yet unknown woman. Her hunger drove Candace to look back to the menu; her head flinched back and forth with the conflicting interests before finally locking onto the menu. She fixed on an item for a moment and then back at the mystery woman. Now the woman looked very distraught and drooped her head toward the table.

The hostess arrived with another couple at the table between Candace's and the unknown woman's. She placed a menu in one place and moved to make room for the woman to sit as she placed the other menu in the opposite setting.

Candace moved her head back and forth to see around the three moving people. The mystery woman covered her face as she broke into tears. Hosea reached for a napkin and pushed it into her hand. The overweight husband sat down at the table between them, totally obscuring Candace's view of the sobbing woman; she moved to Hosea's seat for an unobstructed view. The woman was gasping for air between sobs. Hosea looked from side to side momentarily from the unexpected display of emotion and then back to the woman, putting his hand on her arm to comfort her as he leaned in to continue speaking softly. His words calmed her, and the sobbing subsided.

Candy gawked at the scene with the menu dropping from her hand, wondering, *What is going on here? What did he say to her? Who is that woman?* She looked around the patio at all the people engaged in their meals and conversations. *Does no one else see what is going on here?* she wondered.

The cheerful waitress appeared with the coffee and tea, proclaiming, "Here ya go," and brought Candace's attention back to the table. Having recognized Candace's change of seats and interest across the room, she turned to see the woman crying at the other table. Startled at this event, she looked back at Candace uncomfortably and, not knowing how to respond, asked awkwardly, "Is there anything I can do?"

Flustered by the intrusion, Candace returned her look, nervously reached for the coffee, and said, "No" as she drew it to her lips. Her lips stretched toward the cup, and she sucked a few drops of the steaming liquid into her mouth. She recoiled quickly and nearly spilled it in the process.

"Careful. It's hot," said the waitress. "Are you okay?" she asked, feeling like she had failed by not warning her before she drank. "I'll give you a few more minutes," she said, excusing herself and backing away from the table.

"Thank you," Candace responded as she placed the coffee on the table.

Candace leaned back in the chair, looking toward the crying woman. Her head came up now as she wiped the tears from her face and recomposed herself. She batted her eyes and, with an expression that looked like both laughing and crying, looked Hosea in the eye, and Candace could see her gratefully mouthing, "Thank you." Hosea brushed her dark hair back from her eye, and he pushed his chair back from the table. He rose and reached out his hand toward her. She put her hand in it and looked up at him, smiling as he clasped it with his other hand and squeezed it lightly for a moment before backing up and turning to walk back to Candace, who was still staring at them.

Hosea glided back to the table with the youthful glow of a kid with an ice cream cone. He sat in the seat formerly occupied by his mesmerized wife. Unaffected by her dumbfounded look, he looked back with a broad grin, leaned forward and picked up the menu at his former seat, and glanced from page to page. "I hear they have great apple bread here." Her mouth dropped open, but she stared at him speechless.

The woman returned from the restroom to find her now disheveled friend leaning back in the chair, breathing deeply with a 100-yard stare. Something had obviously happened in her absence, and she paused to survey her friend for a moment and then looked around the courtyard for clues and then back at her friend. Impervious to her friend's return, the woman continued to stare blankly. "Sherie, what happened?" her friend asked.

"Hosea, what just happened over there?" Candace demanded after a moment as she gestured her left hand toward the table with the unknown woman and her friend.

Hosea looked up from the menu and responded as if someone had just introduced a new topic. "What?" he said airily.

"That woman, what did you say to that woman?" she demanded.

"Huh? Oh, uh, I can't say, but I am really hungry. I haven't had eggs benedict for a long time," he continued, pointing at the menu with his toothy grin.

"Wait a minute," Candace insisted. "You just said something to that woman that made her cry. What did you say to her?" not letting him change the subject. "And who is that woman?" she continued with an air of jealousy which Hosea picked up on and forced him to answer.

"Uh, I don't know her name, or, I mean, I *didn't* know her name. Her name is Sherie," he said, laughing nervously. "I didn't know her till just now," he clarified.

Candy glared back at him, insinuating that he should continue speaking.

"She had an old wound that needed to heal, and so God did that for her," he said, shrugging his shoulders.

"What, was she bleeding? What are you talking about? She was just sitting over there enjoying her breakfast, and you went over there and said something that made her cry; she was sobbing."

"That was joy," he retorted, sobering up just a little, and then corrected himself. "At least, it turned to joy. First, she was upset, and then she got healed. God healed a wound she had in her heart, then she got the joy."

"What do you mean, *joy*? People don't cry from joy."

"You've never been to a wedding or a childbirth?" he interrupted. "People cry from joy. I cried when Justice was born," he said, glancing at the quiet stroller for a quick reference.

Candace was shocked, speechless by the explanation, and just stared at him with her mouth open.

"Yes, it hurts when you open the wound, but when the healing comes, the joy rushes in immediately," he said, sweeping his hand, "and captures the pain and carries it away...and...that's how God heals it." He paused to look over to Sherie's table, where she and her friend were happily gathering their purses to leave as if nothing so dramatic had even happened a few moments before. "She's a new person now," he declared and looked back at Candace. "She'll never be the same again," he said confidently, renewing his smile.

Hosea spotted his tea across the table, reached over to pick it up and leaned back in his chair, and took a sip as he peered back into the menu and then put the menu down on the table closed.

Candace followed his lead, picked up the coffee, and

sipped it while staring blankly. Her gaze picked up Sherie and her friend over Hosea's shoulder as they were leaving through the courtyard gate. They were smiling and laughing as they passed through the gate.

Hosea took another sip and said out loud to himself, "I knew there was a good reason to go out to breakfast today," and then smiled at Candace.

She had withdrawn into contemplation. The waitress returned to the table. "Are you ready to order?" she asked cautiously, taking out her pad and pen, glancing back and forth between the two.

"Oh, yeah," answered Hosea eagerly, looking up at her. "I will have the eggs benedict, wheat toast, a small apple juice, and another tea…and the apple bread." He looked across to Candy, who was still despondent and mentally removed from the waitress and her question. Hosea answered for her, looking back at Camille, "She usually likes an omelet with many different kinds of cheese, and a big warm salsa on the side, and milk, and another coffee, and since she doesn't want her toast today, make it wheat, and I'll eat it."

CHAPTER 9—KATIE

During their breakfast, Daniel was energized by his encounter with Sherie and led the conversation, while Candace mostly smiled cordially and went in and out of an apparent preoccupation with some thought that bothered her. He wasn't sure what was happening but noticed that it had started when he returned from his visit with Sherie. By the time they all buckled into the car with Justice abiding peacefully in the back seat, Daniel felt he should ask her what was going on before he started the car. "Hey, honey, what's going on? You look a little…like you're thinking about something. Would you like to talk about it?" he inquired gently.

Candace looked at him for a long moment as she decided if she wanted to share, and Daniel quietly let her go through that process. She leaned back in her seat and looked straight out the windshield before she started. "I was thinking about what you said, about how people cry for joy at weddings, and I remembered being in a wedding when I was a little girl. I was with my sister; we were flower girls, I was three, and she was five, and we went down each side of the aisle, dropping flowers in the aisle before the bride came out, our cousin who was getting married. And we had matching white dresses and gloves and bonnets, and she was a little taller than me, but we looked like twins, everyone always thought we were twins when they first saw us, our whole life, every time we went somewhere people thought we were twins and asked, 'They are so pretty, are they twins?' And my mom would say, 'No, they're twenty-three months apart.' We both had long blonde hair, which my mom kept almost perfect all the time. And we were walking down the aisle, dropping rose petals, but I didn't want to drop the petals because they were so pretty and smelled so good, so my sister and the people I passed were coaching me the whole way to keep moving and keep dropping the petals like my sister. They were all very happy and adoring of us, but I also saw that some of them were crying, they had tears on their cheeks, and they were wiping their eyes with handkerchiefs, and I didn't understand why they were crying." She paused to look at Daniel. "I had forgotten all about that until you said that about crying at weddings, and then I remembered, and now I know why they were crying."

Daniel knew he had touched something deep beyond what she had shared, so he unbuckled his seat belt and turned toward Candace. "I didn't know you had a sister," he prompted.

Candace turned back straight in her seat, looked up to the roof and took a deep breath, and released it slowly.

She closed her eyes and lowered her head, "Yes, I had a sister, Catherine. They called us Katie and Candy. We were practically inseparable." She reminisced, "We looked like twins, we liked all the same things, we did everything together, we wore matching clothes, and we were girly girls. We were one hundred percent girls; there was no tomboy in us at all, zero." She giggled lightly before sharing her next thought, "And my mom had clothes that matched us also, about half the time, all dresses and skirts—no pants, we wore shorts underneath 'for modesty' my mother taught us, and we looked like our mom too." She sobered back up and continued sharing as she stared straight ahead through the windshield. "And that was all great until we were about ten, or she was about ten. I was eight. Because my dad wanted and boy, and we weren't boys, and no boys ever came, so it was just us two girls, and he tried to do boy things with us, but we were just not into any of it. We wouldn't touch a fish—stinky, slimy fish—worms were *totally* gross, and you had to stick that on a hook?" she sneered sarcastically. "My dad brought home a duck once that he shot, and we were horrified, we cried terribly and acted like he was the worst kind of a person, that he would actually kill an animal, a beautiful living duck, he shot it out of the air and brought it home to eat it! We couldn't believe he would actually do that *to a duck,*" she emphasized. "An innocent shiny, green duck. We resented our father for weeks because of that," she remembered. "We wouldn't play football, no baseball, no soccer, no dirt, no mud," she belabored. "We were girls but not just girls—*princesses.* Our mom taught us to be ladies, and we loved it. We fully embraced girliness and despised anything like a boy. *Camping?*" she added indignantly. "No way! And that was great until Katie was about ten, and I don't really know what happened, but maybe he started resenting that. Maybe he didn't realize it, but he started being mean to us." She turned to look at Daniel, shrugging her shoulders and lifting her palms up. "Maybe it was something else. I don't know. He just started being mean, especially to Katie; she got the brunt of it at first. We could go out and do things in public, and he was fairly nice to us, but the rest of the time, he talked down to us, and when our mom tried to help us, he would snap at her." She turned back to lament toward the windshield. "It got worse and worse until when Katie turned fourteen, in the springtime, she ran away." She turned back to explain to Daniel, "We were best friends and then for about a week she just didn't talk to me much, and then one day she just disappeared without a word, no note, nothing. I think she was planning; also, I think she was emotionally distancing herself from me because she didn't want to think about hurting me by leaving." Candace stared back out the window, took a deep breath, and blew it out with a heavy sigh.

"I'm sorry to hear about that, Candace," Daniel empathized. "I can see why you never talked about it."

Candace looked down at her lap soberly. "It gets worse."

Daniel grimaced in anticipation as she continued.

Candace spoke pensively toward the windshield again.

"The police came and talked to us, our friends helped and comforted us, the community looked for her, and her picture was on the TV news and in the newspapers. We figured she ran away, but we didn't know to where; maybe Detroit, Lansing, Grand Rapids. Maybe she was in the country. I don't know. We were looking for about six months, but by wintertime, we weren't expecting much to find her. We just got used to that hole in our hearts. After less than a year, my dad started getting mean again, and I was the only girl left, so it all went to me. It got worse and worse until I didn't want to come home, so one day, when I was fourteen, in the springtime, I didn't go home, just like Katie, no warning, no note, just gone. I thought Katie was out there somewhere, so I went looking for her. I cut my hair, changed my look, and avoided the police. It's amazing how easy it was to hide in plain sight. I didn't know much about how to hide, but they never found me. People are just so involved with themselves that they're not out looking for lost people, I guess. They've got this picture of this girl with long blonde hair with no makeup, and I didn't look like that at all on the first day."

Daniel struggled for words but could only gape in wonder as she continued. He pondered how her mother must have felt having lost her two beautiful daughters, but he feared to voice it; how devastating!

"I didn't know anything about the streets," Candace continued, glancing back at Daniel for a moment, but it was too hard to tell the story and look at him, so she went back to the windshield. "There were lots of people to take advantage of me. They were friendly and helpful enough until they got me alone. That was always the goal, at least for men. They always had drugs and alcohol, and once I got drunk, I was easy to..." She looked down at her knees for a moment. "Once I got on drugs, that helped them a lot because they knew I needed drugs, and they could manipulate me that way. But eventually, I learned how things worked, and I learned how to work the system, to work the people, especially men, because *I* had what *they* wanted. Once I learned that, the tables turned, and I started working *them* in *my* favor." She paused to reflect for a moment. "But the whole time I was looking for Katie, I knew she was out there somewhere. After about a month in Michigan, I didn't think I would find her there anymore, so I started going to other cities in other states. Sometimes I told people I was looking for my sister, who looked like me, but mostly I just looked. I made myself familiar with the city, looked around until I felt I saw everything I could see, and when I determined she wasn't there, I moved on. When it got cold, I moved south. I spent my first winter in Florida," she emphasized logically. "In summer, I went north. Some places were better than others, but everywhere there were men." She felt very uncomfortable talking to Daniel about men, but she felt compelled to finish her story, and it helped to just look out the windshield. "So eventually, after a few years, I ended up in Los Angeles. Nevada was good to me, but I had to go to Los Angeles. For what I was doing, I actually had a lot of good times. Sometimes I would stay for weeks or a month with some rich, single guy who just wanted a pretty woman hanging on his arm and sleeping in his bed, and they happily spent lots of money taking me out to dinner and buying me clothes and jewelry and lingerie, but eventually, something would change, and back on the streets I would go. I learned that when I saw it coming, it was best to make the break as easy as possible. Before they started being mean to me." Her face squinched up, and tears began to flow as she struggled to get out the next words crying, "That's why it's so hard to believe that you've kept me so long, and we even have a baby."

Daniel broke into tears as he reached out to embrace her. They both cried together for a moment, rocking back and forth between the seats before she pushed him away. "Wait, wait, I have to finish; I have to tell you what happened, you need to know, I have to tell you." He reluctantly leaned back on the door as she wiped away her tears with the back of her hand and her nose with her forearm, the mascara leaving trails under her eyes. Daniel wiped his tears with his palms and settled back to hear the rest of her story.

Candace took a couple of deep breaths and turned sideways in her seat to face him before starting again. "So, I ended up in Los Angeles, *which is a big place*," she emphasized. "I went back and forth between the wealthy parts and the tougher parts, looking for Katie and making money. I don't know," she gestured with her hands. "I figured she was on the streets somewhere, but maybe she got married and lived in a house somewhere with her family. I didn't know where she was, but I just kept looking. And so, over time, I learned about this house. This lady had a house near the city, it was where the city started changing into houses, and it had a front yard and a back yard, and in the back, there were fruit trees and shade trees and a porch and swings. It was a pretty big yard for where it was; it was an older house. It felt like an oasis in the city because of the yard. It had four bedrooms and two bathrooms. The master bedroom was hers with one bathroom, the other bathroom was in the hall—every man for himself or actually every woman for herself, and believe me," she said matter-of-factly, "there were some major battles for the bathroom. There were eight beds in the other three rooms, and that bathroom was not made for eight women."

Daniel chuckled with that thought.

"This lady, her name was Janine—Jeanie, we called her—she rented out beds for fifty dollars a night, which was actually a day because most of the women were there sleeping during the day and out at night, although sometimes there were one or two that actually lived there and were reforming their life and helping her out with the house. Jeanie had rules in the house; it had to stay clean, and you had to stay clean. There were no drugs allowed, and if you got caught, she kicked you out for at least twenty-four hours. So, we found places to hide things, but mostly, we just kept them out of the house. If you wanted to smoke cigarettes, it was in the back half of the yard away from the house, and you'd better pack your butts because you couldn't leave them on the ground. I never smoked. Jeanie was a nice lady, but she had rules, and you had to keep the rules, and the house always looked clean. If you ate food, you had to wash the dishes and put them away before you left the kitchen. If you took a bathroom break and came back, you were busted! She had a picture of Jesus on the refrigerator and a bigger picture of Jesus walking on water in the living room. I thought that was strange; a painting of a guy in a robe walking on the choppy water. Sometimes she talked to people about Jesus if they wanted, and she was always trying to help people improve their life. If you stayed there, you couldn't hang out in the front yard. She kept it clear out there, she had grass, and there was a shade tree on one side of the walkway. She spent a lot of time on the porch watching the place and greeting people that went by, and she would only allow one person out there with her at a time *if* she was talking with them. Sometimes I stayed at her house." Candace paused, took a deep breath, and consciously composed herself before continuing.

Daniel could see something big was coming.

"So, this is what I heard happened. Stan had six girls working for him; they were all on heroin. He kept all his girls on heroin so he could control them. He was always sober, right, a businessman. One day he had heroin coming before they went out for the night, and the guy was late; they were waiting for him. It came, but it was bad stuff." She paused, closed her eyes, took another deep breath, and blew it out slowly. "They all took it, and they were all dead within an hour. Six women were dead in the apartment. Stan had a problem. I heard that the delivery boy disappeared after that, but Stan had a problem. He had all the girls dumped at different places in the city, and I don't know how he did it, but he never got busted for this. The police found them all; it made the news, six women in one night within a couple of miles. But they never traced those girls back to him, somehow, and that runner disappeared, that's seven dead, and Stan got away with it. But Stan needed more women; all his girls were gone. So, he had heard about this house on the other side of the city where the girls stayed, Jeanie's house, so he called the police about the house and at ten o'clock in the morning when all the girls were sleeping, the police raided the house and took all the girls but Jeanie, even a good one. I don't know how he did this because the house was clean, there were no drugs in the house, but all those girls got busted." Candace paused for a breath. "And I was one of those girls."

Daniel gasped, but he dared not interrupt.

Candace closed her eyes tightly, grimacing, and shuttered before she continued slowly. "Stan was out there watching when we came out of the house, none of us saw him, but he was somewhere, watching. He picked out six of us, girl for girl. He went downtown and bailed us all out, the ones he wanted. The police let us go, and being grateful and feeling an obligation to return the favor, we went home with Stan. I had no idea what was happening. I never heard of Stan, and I didn't know who he was. Two of the girls knew about him, and I noticed they were scared, but I didn't let that bother me. I thought I could take care of myself; I had always managed to stay free from that kind of pimp. I thought that I would just thank Stan for his help, return the favor in some way and be on my way, but that's not what happened." Candace slowed down and spoke every word deliberately, almost like a robot, so she could get through it, trembling. Her eyes swelled as she continued, "I never got out of there. In a week, I was hooked on heroin; in two weeks, I thought I would be trapped there forever. After a month, I felt so hopeless; I just wanted to die." She fell into sobbing as she finished, "I wanted to die every day after that, but he wouldn't let me die. I was his slave."

Daniel lunged forward, weeping, and wrapped his arms around her.

She continued fighting her pain and her joy to finish her story with her chin on his shoulder. "Until that day that you came and rescued me, I was his slave."

As Daniel held her there weeping, with the pain, remorse, hatred, contempt, comfort, and love sweeping through him in waves, he never wanted to let her go. They just cried there together for a long while until Justice started crying, and they had to give him their attention. At that time, Daniel didn't know if Katie was dead or alive, but he secretly determined in his heart to find her.

CHAPTER 10—FAST FOOD PROPHECY

Early one afternoon, as Hosea was driving the SUV with Candace and baby Justice, a sudden discomfort overtook him. They were driving quietly down a local parkway when his demeanor tensed, his eyes furled and squinted while he began scanning the shops and stores on both sides of the road. Candace noticed the abrupt new tension and movement, followed his eyes to see what he was looking for and when she couldn't tell what bothered him, she inquired, "What's the matter?"

"I'm not sure, but something's wrong," he replied with a tense agitation.

"Wrong with what?" she asked with concern.

"I don't know, but it's coming up around here somewhere," he continued. "I'll know when I see it."

Puzzled by the sudden change of events, Candace continued to watch him until his steely gaze locked onto a fast-food burger restaurant coming up on the righthand side of the road. His intensity increased as he squealed into the lot, parked abruptly, and, without a word, opened the car door and slammed it shut as if he had forgotten that his family was with him, and he started marching toward the front door.

"What's going on?" she shouted through the glass in a panic.

He turned like he was surprised to see her there, shook his head and batted his eyes as if she had no reason to be upset, and then blurted out, "Don't worry, this should only take a minute." He turned and marched resolutely toward the entrance. A few seconds later, he disappeared through the swinging glass doors, leaving Candace stupefied in the car.

As the door swung closed behind him, he stopped to scan the restaurant with his steely glare before locking onto a man seated by himself on a bench along the wall at a small table. The man was an average-looking guy with short brown hair, a white complexion, maybe five feet and ten inches, and normal weight. He had his back to the wall, facing out toward the open restaurant. He was lifting half a hamburger to his face when Hosea marched toward his table and, with an extended arm and index finger stopping just short of his table, leaned toward him and trumpeted his declaration, "You, sir, need to go home right now and apologize to your wife." His voice sounded loudly through the restaurant.

The surprised man froze in his seat with the burger inserted in his mouth, his eyes wide open, looking at Hosea, all of the chatter ceased, and every eye of the busy lunchtime crowd turned in his direction.

Hosea continued with all authority, "You have yelled at that woman for the last time. She has served you and those three kids of yours every day without complaint for eight years while you have cursed and berated her almost continually that whole time for no good reason. She cooked your food, had your babies, changed your diapers, prayed for you every day, and now you think you can just throw her away like trash." Hosea retracted his arm, stood up straight, put his hands on his waist, and took on a sassy, mocking tone as the patrons gawked in amazement, "And what are you going to do? Go rent an apartment, visit your kids on the weekend, make your own food, do your own laundry, and pay all your ex-wife's bills? When the whole time, you had a good woman that you took for granted, mistreated, and used as you pleased. If you did that, you would be one sorry mutt." He paused before starting back in matter-of-factly, "But you're not gonna do that because this is your last chance. God sent me here today to give you (raising his index finger) one last chance to repent before you destroy your life and He gives your woman to a better man who will raise those kids in fear of God and the love they deserve. You know what you need to do." Hosea paused for a second before leaning back in and extending his finger just inches from the man's nose while the man's eyes crossed to focus on the incoming fingertip. Hosea continued with slightly less thunder into a final demand, "Now you humble yourself to God and repent, go back to your wife and beg for mercy and forgiveness, and you respect her as the virtuous woman she is. You go back to that church you left over a year ago, you apologize to that pastor for your words and your attitude and ask him to teach you how to be a good father, and *you* do *everything* he tells you to do." Hosea stared at the man for a moment, his demeanor lightened, and he took on a radiant smile as he made his final decree, "God has a great plan for your life, Ryan." Hosea turned and, still oblivious to all of the people in the room, marched back to the door and left just as abruptly as he had come in.

The bewildered customers watched the prophet go out the door and then turned back to look at the man, his mouth brimming with the burger. He put down the food, lowered his eyes, and dropped his head.

Candace was watching the restaurant door as Hosea emerged only moments after he had disappeared. His face beamed with joyous energy as he approached the car. He waved happily at Candace about halfway there, her eyes widened, and her mouth dropped open in disbelief. He opened the door and bounced into the car, strapped into his seat, and announced jubilantly, "Okay, we can go now," as Candace looked on speechless. He started the car, surveyed his intended path, and headed back out to the street.

Once he had gotten back on the road, Candace overcame her shock enough to ask, "What just happened?"

***

As the sun dipped down onto the horizon later that day in a mature, urban, track home neighborhood, Ryan made his way up the walkway to his house. He had a dozen dark red roses in his left hand and a box of Courtney's favorite chocolates under the same arm. As he approached the door, his knees got weak, his body trembled, and his eyes started pumping out tears which streamed down his cheeks and fell to the ground. When he got to the door, he reached out his fist and made his signature knock.

His wife was sitting on the couch in the shadowy front room, bent forward with her face buried in her hands, when she heard the familiar knock. Surprised by the sound, she lifted her head and wiped her red nose with a wadded-up tissue. With puffy, swollen eyes, she looked at the door in disbelief and around the empty room. When the knock came a second time, she got up from the couch and cautiously walked to the door. She opened it slowly to see Ryan standing there, tears streaming down his face. She had never seen him like that before. Looking her straight in the eyes, with quivering lips and a broken voice, he whimpered, "Will you please forgive me?"

She gasped lightly as a sense of life and hope swept back into her heart.

CHAPTER 11—BABY GRACE

Several months after Justice was born, Candace found herself pregnant again. They reasoned it was a result of the camping trip they went on; they didn't remember *all* of the supplies they were supposed to bring. Candace later thought that maybe it wasn't an accident after all and that the camping food, especially that stuff he referred to as "chili," wasn't what made her sick the next morning after all. She eventually surmised that two nights in a tent was Daniel's secret recipe for another baby. But when she started suspecting she was pregnant, she wasn't upset; she was overjoyed. She tried to surprise him, but when he saw that joyful glow she was wearing, he figured it out before she could tell him. It was impossible news to hide. When he got home for dinner that night a few weeks after the camping trip, the way she looked when she greeted him said it all. That special, deep, quiet expression of joy could only come from a baby. They spent most of that evening on the couch, doting over each other and the baby on the way.

Daniel already had a name for her, even before the

camping trip, but he let Candace buy a name book and go through the name picking procedure until she found the name he wanted. They both enjoyed the process; for him, it was more about the journey than the destination since he already had the name. When Candace started contemplating the name *Grace* from the list, he just said, "I like that, we can name her Candace Grace, but we'll call her Grace." That was all Candace needed, she breezed through the book a few more times, but the search was over.

Grace came about nine months after the camping trip. Candace had a textbook pregnancy, as Dr. Leafman called it; a few crazy food cravings in the night—thank God for the food deliverers, but Daniel still had to walk out to the front gate in the rain after midnight once. Candace became increasingly grumpier, uncomfortable, that is, as her stomach grew and she advanced into a waddle. Grace came on the original expected delivery date, and this time, they even made it to the delivery room before giving birth. Three pushes, and there she was; Candace Grace Freeman.

CHAPTER 12—THE LITTLE FOXES

Daniel and Candace enjoyed seafood appetizers amongst other diners amidst the smattering of tables, high ceilings, chandeliers, and white tablecloths and curtains as they waited for the main dishes to arrive at their table. Daniel always made sure they got out for at least one meal to a nice restaurant during the week for just the two of them. On the weekends, they often entertained their children, friends, or business associates at night, so the weekday break kept their relationship warm and alive. The restaurants weren't crowded on Tuesdays, so they never had to wait to get in without a reservation which meant they could choose a place on the spur of the moment; the rare spontaneity of choice was also refreshing. Daniel continued the conversation as Candace raised another shrimp to her mouth. "So, Justice slipped and fell on his butt in the chocolate milk after he dumped it on the floor?" he asked jovially, looking straight across the table at her.

She rolled the shrimp into her cheek and continued her story, "Yes, I hadn't put the top on it yet, and he was just barely able to touch it enough to knock it off the counter, and I heard it bounce off his head and hit the floor..."

Daniel lanced a scallop with his fork and put it in his mouth, enjoying the story.

"...I turned around and saw that surprised look on his face for a moment before he focused on *me*, and then he started crying and stuck his arms straight out towards me, and he didn't even get one step—"

Daniel picked up the story as if he had been there to watch it, "When his feet flew out from under him, and he landed flat on his butt."

"Splat!" she finished the story, and they both chuckled. A stately gentleman across the room glanced in their direction with a raised brow. Their conversation had escalated to a little more excitement than the posh bistro was used to, and as they adjusted down to the prevailing ambiance, the phone buzzed in his shirt pocket. He looked at the screen and then at Candace, pointing, "It must be the kids; it's Claire." Now conscious of the few other people in the restaurant, he pushed his chair back and slipped away to talk.

Candace smiled mirthfully as she reminisced the story and speared the last scallop for herself. She leaned back and relished the flavor for a moment, rolling it over her tongue from cheek to cheek. Daniel was out of sight, and the appetizer plate was empty, so she began looking around the dining room. A beautiful woman with wavy long blonde hair across the room in her elegant flowing white dress was sitting adjacent to her handsome, well-groomed, black-haired husband. At first, she thought, *A slightly mature Barbie and Ken. No, it was closer to Scarlet O'Hara and Rhett Butler. No, it was Barbie and Rhett thrown together from their respective eras in a contrast of dark and light hair and wardrobe.* Barbie had a brilliant flowing mane and a radiant pearl necklace. The living doll reached for her glass and took a sip of her wine. Rhett continued to talk as she rolled the wine around in the glass, admiring its color and texture. Barbie let it settle in the glass and then slowly took another sip. She savored the wine more than Candace had savored that last scallop, it seemed. It certainly looked as if Barbie was enjoying her wine more than Candace had enjoyed those succulent seafood morsels. Then Rhett followed her lead and took a sip from his glass. He motioned his glass toward Barbie, she lifted her glass, tipped it toward him, and then they both drank in unison, eyes fixed on each other as they drank.

A waiter passed by Candace's table, and the movement shifted her eyes toward another couple. Their waiter, on the other side of their table, facing Candace, lifted their bottle of wine from the ice bucket and refilled their chalices, lady first, as they looked on. These were as elegant as the first two, but their hair was silver, and his face was tan and weathered, but hers was porcelain and smooth as if kissed by one of the world's most accomplished plastic surgeons and nurtured by the finest exotic creams. Candace reached for her water and sipped it as if imitating the wine drinkers, but the water now tasted worse than the tap at her house.

She stretched it out away from her and looked at it with one disdainful eye. She knew this was the finest spring water one could buy, but it had lost its flavor. She set it down with a painful frown. She continued looking around the room from table to table. She noticed that every table had wine except hers. Every couple seemed to be enjoying themselves, loosened by its influence and mellowed from the day's labors. They were enjoying themselves more than she was at that moment, or so she thought. Deceived by the seductive, dancing, fermented juices, Candace was scowling at her water when Daniel returned to the table. He happily whispered in her direction that she had left the diapers in the car after shopping, presumably because of the chocolate milk spill, and Claire couldn't find any in the house, so they worked it out over the phone during his absence from the table. "Is anything wrong?" he asked as he sat in his seat, sensing the change of atmosphere and the fall of Candace's countenance since he had left the table.

"No," she said, regaining composure, shaking the scowl from her face and replacing it with a sufficiently engaging smile. An aroma filled the air just before the waiter silently appeared from behind her with a small folding table and a covered platter, which he placed next to their table before removing the lid. Their eyes widened, and the festivity revived as steak, fish, and a variety of intricate works of culinary art were strategically placed under their noses.

The waiter bowed and asked, "Is there anything else I

can get for you?"

"No, thank you," replied Daniel as he replaced the napkin on his lap and tilted his head toward the waiter, encouraging him to leave. There was a quiet active moment as they both moved on to their main courses. Their taste buds were again excited, and their noses flared as the heavenly aromas arose before them. They sunk their knives and forks into the steak and fish as quickly as dignity would allow in such a bistro. After they had both swallowed the first bite, they started to speak simultaneously, laughed, and then simultaneously said, "You first," and then laughed a little harder, then Daniel quickly inserted a bite of food in his mouth, indicating that it was her turn to talk.

"I want to know what *you* did today," she interjected as he chewed. "What kind of deals were you feeling?"

"Feeling?" he said inquisitively, trying to think what she meant by that, then he captured the memory of their first car ride to his desert racetrack. "Oh yeah, *feeling*." He paused. That memory and that person had almost been erased from his mind. Why had it suddenly emerged in this conversation at this moment?

"Yes, *feeling*," she playfully prodded.

Daniel was unexplainably stumped by the question, which led to an awkward silence as he tried to think of any decision he had made that day by explicitly *feeling* something. The concept of *feeling* zipped through his mind as he recounted every event of the day as they dashed by in order. *I felt good all day; I was happy*, he thought. *Did I make a decision based purely on feeling?* A waft of fish brought him back to the meal and partially out of his contemplation. He cut off another piece and put it in his mouth. After a moment, he said matter-of-factly and slightly aloof, "I don't recall *feeling* anything."

Of course, the intended meaning of *feeling* had escaped; it was funny in the original conversation those few years ago, as she remembered it. Candace didn't know why she had chosen to say that, but it certainly had quenched the conversation, and she didn't know why. Attempting to bring back the levity, she resorted back to the spill. "So yeah, I was bringing the food from the car when that little accident happened, so that's why the diapers were left behind. I had to clean the little guy up and get him some more milk."

Daniel got back on track, nodding in agreement as he leaned into his next cut of fish, and the smile returned to his face. "I'm sure he needed some love after that," he chuckled.

"Love, attention, new pants, a few kisses, and finally another chocolate milk sippy cup. That's when things really got better." Candace was relieved she had saved the conversation. She continued, "You'll never guess what Grace did today that was so funny."

"Okay, what did *she* do?" Daniel asked with renewed excitement, wondering what new thing his baby girl had done while he was away for the day.

"Okay," Candace giggled, trying to swallow a bite before she started the story. "So, I fed her, and then I tried to burp her, but she wouldn't burp, and I was a little concerned because she always burps pretty quickly, so then I finally gave up and laid her down, and Claire and I were looking at her for a minute and talking about it, and then we both turned to walk away, and we heard this giant belch. We both looked at each other with big saucer eyes and turned around and looked down at her, and she was looking back up at us, and then she just started laughing, and then we started laughing."

"My belching baby girl," Daniel said as if introducing an entertainer to an awaiting audience.

"She sounded like a grown man who just guzzled a beer!" said Candace trying to muffle her excitement. "We couldn't believe it!"

"Such a big burp from that little baby," Daniel chuckled.

"She is getting big. Actually, she's getting fat!" she said with actuating eyes.

Daniel matched her widening eyes, "I know, in the last week, she looks like she's grown three belt notches."

"Mmm, maybe two weeks, but yes, she is getting fat. I noticed about two weeks ago she's been growing out instead of up."

"She's getting ready for another growth spurt; she's saving up. She grows out before she grows up," Daniel surmised happily.

"I'm sure she is; she beats every marker, that's for sure.

She's going to pass up Justice real soon if she keeps up this pace," Candace chided.

"Girls grow faster than boys," Daniel shrugged and lifted his fork and knife. Grace's growth had sparked a friendly boy/girl competition between the couple as they vicariously competed against each other through their kids. Daniel seemed to be conceding to his inevitable defeat when his younger girl would pass his older boy on the growth chart. "But he'll catch up later," he assured himself out loud.

The boisterous couple did not quite fit into the hushed and calm protocol of this restaurant. They talked a little louder, ate a little faster, and showed a little more excitement than the other guests. They were reminded to tone down again when the waiter arrived at their table, addressing Daniel, "Is there anything else you would like this evening?" he asked.

"No, thank you, sir," replied Daniel jovially but respectfully acknowledging the waiter's intent.

The waiter turned to Candace, "Anything to drink, ma'am?" He seemed to her like a child who had just heard *no* from one parent and then petitioned the other.

To drink, she thought for a second, gazing at the waiter in silence.

"No, thank you," interrupted Daniel, mildly scolding the disobedient child. "We've got to get home to our children."

"Then, I'll be back in a moment with your check,"

concluded the waiter.

"Thank you," nodded Daniel as the waiter bowed and stepped away. Daniel leaned back in his chair and folded his hands over his belly, looking at his wife but thinking about his children.

Candace leaned back in her chair and folded her hands on her belly, looking at Daniel but thinking about sipping some wine.

CHAPTER 13—SOAP AT THE NAIL SHOP

Candace opened the door to the manicure boutique for her bi-weekly manicure and surveyed the room for an empty seat. The woman behind the counter interrupted her scan warmly, "Hi, Candace, how are you doing today? You're looking good. Are you ready for a new color today?"

"I'm doing it all today, honey. Where do you want me? It looks pretty busy," she replied sassily.

"Yes, it is, but look, we have a seat for you right over here," pointing to the middle-aged woman who was exiting a chair while looking at her nails, spreading her fingers, and flipping her hands back and forth with a well-satisfied grin on her face. Candace moved toward the chair, passing by the lady who looked like she had also been to the hair salon before this.

Candace took her seat and greeted her manicurist cheerfully, "Good afternoon, Sophi. How are you doing today?"

"Oh, I'm wonderful as always. I'm happy to see you

here today, right on time," replied Sophi.

"Yes, two weeks; I'm ready for a whole new look. I want to go fire engine red this week," she announced with an air of risqué.

"Whoa! Feeling frisky, huh?"

"Something like that, just want a little change and do something bold," Candace surmised as she settled into the seat and realized that she was looking right over Sophi's shoulder at the television. She noted that she had never sat in that chair before with the TV dominating her view. It was the top of the hour, so a string of commercials was running as she settled into her seat. The last time she was there she couldn't even see the TV. Everyone had been watching *Let's Make a Deal*, and she couldn't see it. It was family day, and a couple of surfers had made it to the main event. She could hear what was going on but couldn't see, and everyone was talking about the cute little girl in her baggy surf shorts, rash guard with zinc stripes under her eyes and on her nose. "What a cute little girl!" they chorused as she and her father stepped down to the stage. "I hope she wins," one of the customers added, thoughtlessly dismissing the presence of her father. Candace couldn't move because Stella was painting her nails and wouldn't let her get up, but she could hear Wayne Brady going through the process with them of picking one of the doors. Finally, Candace escaped the chair and raced to see the eight-year-old little blonde and her dad just before the show ended. *They didn't win the car*, she lamented internally, *but they did get some surfboards and wetsuits.* "Well, they got what they came for, I guess," she broadcast to the other onlookers as she headed back to her seat. "That little girl was adorable," she agreed. That was two weeks ago.

Sophi was not as vocal as some of the other ladies in the shop, but she did smile a lot and seemed to enjoy her work. "Hey, honey, is this the color you want?" she asked with a bright little red bottle suspended in the air between them.

"That's exactly it," affirmed Candace before putting a mask on her face to stifle the chemical odors in the room.

"I thought that was it," boasted the manicurist.

The next show, a soap opera, had started while she settled into her seat, and Sophi had started cleaning her nails from the now fading pink from her last visit. On TV, a trio of women seated in a spacious upper-middle-class family room was talking together. "Don't even worry about it," said a woman with an overabundance of long, puffy brown hair. "The courts always favor the women," she proclaimed matter-of-factly.

"Yeah, you'll get the kids most of the time, and he'll get them on weekends, maybe a couple of hours during the week," chimed in a blonde woman with half as much hair falling just past her shoulders.

A woman with a jet-black bob pointing down to her chin picked up next. "All I do is make food, wash dishes and clothes, drive kids around from here to there. I want a life of my own," she declared. "I used to have fun; I *never* get to go to a party or spend a night out on the town with my girlfriends like I used to," she complained.

"Yes, and guys have this big ego thing where they always have to be in charge of everything, and we are just supposed to fall into line and do whatever they tell us; that is such garbage. Women aren't even allowed to have an opinion," continued the blonde lady.

"Yeah, I want to get out and party like I used to; it's been way too long since I got to spend a night out on the town with my *girl*friends," lamented the black bob lady.

"But divorce wrecks the kids; you need to think about that," retorted a fourth woman with long black hair and a light Latina accent entering the room as she returned to her place on the sofa with a cup of coffee. "What did you think was going to happen when you got married and started a family? You have kids because you wanted them, and the kids need a father if they're going to turn out right. Divorce causes a lot of heartache for everyone, *especially* the kids. Kent is a good man, he makes more than enough money for you to get everything you want, and he loves his kids. I think you're just being selfish because you're spoiled, and you *still* don't get everything you want."

"Maria, *everything* is a big word," retorted the bob lady seeking to justify herself. "The one thing I don't have is *freedom*; my life is already decided for me from sunrise to sunset and even at night."

"And is that a bad thing?" Maria interrupted.

"It is after several years of it!" retorted the blonde.

"You're just looking for trouble," Maria continued. "You sound like a dumb teenager, haven't you grown up yet?" she taunted.

"Oh, yeah, I'd like to get into trouble for once; it's been a long time!" the bob lady chided, and then the three all laughed together while Maria shook her head in disagreement.

"It's been a long time since *any* of us got into trouble; getting in trouble used to be a lot of fun," said the blonde. "Don't worry, you'll be the queen bee calling your own shots, and he'll be the worker bee bringing you the check, so you can care for the kids during the week and then go out on the weekends and have fun while *he's* got the kids. You can let him have the kids Friday afternoon till Monday morning, and the court will give it to you because he's got to work all week to pay for the kids, but he's also got to see his kids; that's how it always works."

"Yeah, you'll get the house, and he'll get some little apartment close to work," said the woman with the big brown hair. "And the kids can sleep on the couch when they visit him. They can have fun all weekend, and you can be out on the town all night and sleep on Saturday, Sunday, and Monday. Just be there on time to get them from school on Monday afternoon."

"Yeah, it sounds good here on the couch but living it is another thing," reasoned Maria. "You're going to miss your man before long, and you'll just be looking for another. There's nothing wrong with the one you got now."

"Hey, it's kinda stuffy in here; let's go outside and get some fresh air," said the bob woman, alluding to Maria's negativity toward her plans. "Let's go out on the deck."

"That sounds good, Elly; let's do that," said the blonde as they all started moving from their seats in that direction. Their exit led into a commercial break with a woman mopping a floor.

When the commercial came, Candace shook her head as if she had suddenly awoken from a dream. She focused for a moment on the woman working quietly on her nails, then she surveyed the room and came back to the TV commercial and closed her eyes, blocking it out and recessing deep into thought. She had been mesmerized by the drama. *What a crazy show*, she thought. *That woman is going to leave her husband and kids, so she can party? What a stupid thing to do. Those other women are trying to talk her into it also. I wonder what is so bad about her husband. Nothing! She just wants to party and have him pay for it. I would never do that, leave my husband and kids and all the cool stuff I have and that big house and car,* cars. *He chauffeurs me around in a Ferrari at least once or twice a week. How stupid would that be?*

***

Driving home from the manicure, Candace couldn't stop thinking about the soap opera drama. *People pay for those shows so they can run mop commercials and sell soap and other junk to housewives*, she thought with agitation as she drove. *Those actors get paid big bucks telling their soapbox stories, so someone can come on and sell people soap, sell* women *soap. I couldn't do that anyway. I signed that paper saying that he gets the kids if we divorce. I think that's what it said. I don't know exactly; I never read it. I just saw that handsome man in those nice clothes in that professional-looking car, and I didn't want to be Stan's slave anymore. Stan, whatever happened to Stan? I'm sure he went to jail, maybe he got out, maybe he's dead by now. Daniel just told me what it said; I never even read it. I signed it without even reading it. That was pretty dumb, but I'm glad I did it. That was the best decision I made in my life! That was an awesome deal. Talk about "Let's Make a Deal"; that deal didn't cost me anything. I didn't lose either. I didn't get any little consolation prize—I won the* grand *prize!*

The bob-lady's voice chimed into her thoughts unexpectedly, "You just lost your freedom," she jingled.

Candace stopped at a traffic light and stared blankly at the car ahead of her. Her thoughts changed direction. *How did he pick me anyway? What kind of a guy just drives downtown and picks up a prostitute to marry and have kids with? That is weird. He had that contract all made up before he got there, all typed up and printed out, ready to sign. He had it all planned out in advance. How did he...* the car behind her honked, alerting her back to the light which had just turned green. The cars ahead of her were gone, and she glanced in the rearview mirror quickly before accelerating.

CHAPTER 14—WANDERLUST

Candace continued to think about the women in the soap opera. Their words rolled around in her mind like a marble on a roulette wheel, but the wheel never stopped. The game she now played is called *freedom*. She now found herself agreeing with the show majority and arguing against Maria, the lone voice of reason in the group, just as she had seen on the television. She had more than any of those women had, their stage was an upper-middle-class home, but she had much more than that. She had a bigger house, better cars, a very rich husband, and more beautiful children, she imagined, but she didn't have her freedom. Freedom seemed to come at a higher price for her, but it was still freedom. Her newly developing quest seemed almost patriotic.

He had this whole thing planned out from the beginning, she thought, hardening her heart against her husband and her children. *He had that contract all figured out before he ever met me; he didn't even know who I was, just an easy target. Just find some random prostitute on the streets and wave some dollars in her face, and she'll sign anything. Those were never my children; I never had any rights to them. They were always his; he bought them. I only signed up for one anyway. He tricked me into having two, but there's no way I'm having three.* As these thoughts crowded her mind, she yearned for her husband and children but suppressed those conflicting emotions for her more noble cause; freedom.

What would I do with my freedom? she thought. At first, she had no idea what she would do. She had a great life caring for her children, spending time with her husband, and happily running her house with Juanita's help. What would she do? The concept only created a void in her mind. She had everything a woman could want. But there, in that vacuum, thoughts started creeping in from her past. So many times in that dingy apartment or out on the streets, she would dream about what she would do if she just had some money and could escape from Stan. Her life would be an endless party. She could go to the fancy clubs she had heard about but could not get in; she didn't make the cut, and they would know it. Especially that *one*, "The Wall." It was just a big wall with a door in it. But her friends said that behind the wall was a posh nightclub where the rich and beautiful went to party every night of the week. That's where she saw herself. Her beauty was wasted there on the streets. If she could just escape Stan and get a nice dress, a *really* nice, expensive, fire engine red dress, and a dynamic wavy hairstyle and vibrant makeup, she could get in there, and once she got in there, with all those rich, handsome men, something good would happen for her. She wasn't sure what, but something good would happen.

Life on the street was like chasing a rainbow. There was always that dream, that faint hope that you could escape to somewhere other than the nightmare you were living in. But the rainbow was always somewhere off in the distance, elusive. It was there but intangible. Beyond the rainbow was a normal life with a house and kids and a ring on your finger from someone you loved and who cared for you, who would come home at the end of the day and embrace you and kiss you and tell you that he could never make it without you, and how thankful he was to have you in his life. But that was so far away from their reality that they couldn't even think that far out; they could never get past the rainbow. There was just a faint rainbow out there somewhere past the city buildings and apartments. They knew there was a world out there full of people who had found the rainbow's treasure, but Candy was held back by invisible chains, shackles on her feet and her arms, and around her neck, keeping her from going only so far from her bed. The chain was tied to a bed, and before it could ever stretch to its end, Stan would pull on it and reel her back in. She could never get too far from Stan; he always knew where she was. Sometimes in her stupor, she would forget about him, but then he would suddenly appear, and she always felt like she was in trouble. The chains were invisible, but Stan was not. He always had his hand on her chain. He was sober, sharp-witted, and always one step ahead of everyone else, with so many chains on each finger tied to so many women. He was a businessman; she was just one of his chickens.

On top of that were the drugs. She needed the heroin because she was addicted, and if she didn't have it, she would get sick. That's how Stan knew she would always come back. Because if she ever had pretenses of leaving, she knew that he always had the drugs that she needed. Whenever she would start feeling sick, she could come to him. But they also helped escape the pain, the heartache, the loneliness, the rejection. The drugs weren't bad as long as you didn't run out. They made you feel good, and she knew there were lots of successful men who took the drugs and managed perfectly well in their businesses and made lots of money, and nobody knew they took drugs. At least that's what she imagined.

CHAPTER 15—THE WINE DEBATE

As they drove home from their date one night, Candace couldn't stop thinking about all the people drinking wine with their dinner. As always, she and Daniel were the only ones in the restaurant not drinking alcohol. She felt left out—like she was excluded from the party. Finally, she couldn't resist but ask Daniel the question with a complaining tone, "Why don't we drink wine like everyone else?" she whined.

He looked at her from the corner of his eye, considering the complaint in her voice, "Why should we drink wine? We don't need wine," he answered with a calm assurance.

"I don't know," she said somewhat sheepishly. "Jesus drank wine; it can't be all that bad," she postulated.

"Yeah, well, there's a lot of details there that you have to dig a little deeper to see," he continued.

"Like what?" she jabbed.

Daniel sensed the rise in tension in her voice, "Well, let's start with the obvious. Jesus was a Jew, right?"

"Right," she agreed.

137

"And Jews have certain dietary guidelines outlined in the Bible which we refer to today as..." he paused to let her fill in the blank.

"As...?" repeated Candace, not understanding his intention.

"As kosher," Daniel said, finishing his sentence.

"As kosher," she mimicked, still trying to grasp the concept.

"So, kosher food can be a lot different than what we're used to in some ways. They don't eat pork and other foods that a lot of people like to eat."

"We don't eat pork either," Candace asserted.

"Right, that's because pork is bad for us; that's why God tells us to stay away from it (Leviticus 11:7–8). Anyway, kosher wine is a *lot* different than what most people at restaurants like to drink. For instance, a big factor in that is the alcohol content. Kosher wine usually has a much lower alcohol content as opposed to the other stuff everyone else likes to drink. You would get sick from overeating before you got a little buzz. Obviously, I'm not a wine expert; I don't drink it, my family never drank it, but that's a start." He thought for a moment before lamenting, "Unfortunately, all you need is a rabbi to oversee the wine-making process and bless it, and I've heard that some of the modern rabbis are getting more liberal and allowing higher alcohol content," he said, tapering off and then becoming more assertive. "The biggest thing is that people drink wine to get drunk. The Bible gives us a lot of warnings about getting drunk, starting back with Noah (Genesis 9:20). We see problem after problem, warning after warning." (Proverbs 23:29–35, 31:4–5.)

"Okay, but what about Jesus?" she retorted.

"Okay, I'm getting there. One important thing to know is that the Bible's word for wine and grape juice is the same. The only way to discern juice from wine is by the context. So, when the Bible says Jesus made water into wine, it doesn't mean there was any alcohol in it, and He certainly didn't make it to get everyone drunk; that would be contrary to every biblical principle." He jested, "Saving the best wine for last doesn't mean it had the highest alcohol content." (John 2:10.)

"But isn't a *little* wine okay?" Candace volleyed, hoping to justify her position.

"It's not okay for me; why should I risk getting drunk? Why should I risk other people getting drunk because they see me drinking it, but they don't know when to stop? Here's the biggest thing, the Bible says in Ephesians to not be drunk with wine but be filled with the Spirit (Ephesians 5:18). It looks to me like we have a choice, either one or the other; I like being filled with the Holy Spirit. People filled with wine get cirrhosis of the liver; people full of the Holy Ghost get healed of liver diseases (Matthew 4:23). People filled with wine get stupid (Proverbs 23:33); people filled with the Holy Ghost get wise. People filled with wine have moral failures; people filled with the Holy Spirit keep themselves from sin. People full of wine—"

"Okay, okay, okay, that's enough," Candace interrupted with growing impatience. "So why does everyone talk about Jesus drinking wine?"

"Because they want to get drunk. Why don't they just drink grape juice? Let's face it, they just want to get buzzed, and like the freeway signs say, 'Driving buzzed is driving drunk,' they just want to get drunk, and they say whatever it takes to help them feel justified. There is not even the slightest indication that Jesus ever got drunk or led anyone to get drunk. The community that He lived in was dedicated to purity and holy living. Look at Mary and Joseph and Elizabeth and Zacharias and John the Baptist and the Jewish laws. They took every precaution to make absolutely sure no one got drunk."

"But they had prostitutes then also," she interjected desperately.

"Not at their house," he shot back. "Jesus didn't put anyone in prostitution either; He got them out. He did not create alcoholics; He freed people from alcoholism, 'Go and sin no more,' that's what He said to the prostitutes and the drunks." (John 8:11.)

Candace got quiet as she contemplated other rhetoric to turn the argument in her favor. Daniel looked back and forth between her and the road. He had won the argument, it seemed, but he was more concerned about Candace and why they just had the little foray over wine. That was the closest thing they had ever had to an argument since he met her. He was compelled to share more.

"You have to understand that, over the past two thousand years, people have learned how to increase the alcohol content in wine and other alcohol. The most powerful alcohol in Jesus' day was close to two percent alcohol content, and within the culture of the people dedicated to holiness, they would water that down to make sure no one got drunk. Imagine a strong drink being three percent max. What the people are drinking in the restaurant is closer to twenty percent alcohol, I think. Twenty percent alcohol is going to get you drunk a whole lot faster than watered-down two percent alcohol, right?"

"...Right," Candace agreed reluctantly, conceding to his reasoning before receding back into contemplation. She didn't know enough about the history of wine to refute his argument, but that didn't stop her from wanting to drink it.

CHAPTER 16—THE GRACE DEBATE

As time went on, Candace's discontentment began to grow. Instead of being the sponge eager to take in new information and grow in it, she began to question everything that she had previously learned about her newfound faith. She began looking for more liberal views on the things she had learned, perspectives that allowed her more personal freedom. She began to see the moral fences erected for her protection as barriers that stifled her mobility. She started finding private time to listen to other opinions when not under the watchful eyes of Daniel and Juanita. The Christian radio became her sanctuary to seek out other perspectives less stringent than Daniel's. There she learned from popular preachers new definitions for the terms that Daniel and Juanita had taught her. The first topic that got her attention was grace. As she listened to contemporary messages that both subtly and overtly communicated grace as a celestial license to do whatever she wanted while still protected by a shield of God's unwavering love and forgiveness, she became convinced that her position on alcohol and a growing list of other things was right. The onerous rules that Daniel imposed upon her were far too stringent and stifling; no one is perfect, and Daniel's quest for moral purity is simply irrelevant in light of God's overriding posture of unwavering forgiveness. How could a loving God condemn anyone to hell? She chorused with her new set of mentors. As Candace continued to expand her list of acceptable behavior, the once narrow path to salvation became broader and broader.

As the family sat at the small round dining table one night, with Daniel enjoying the presence of his wife and children, he asked four-year-old Justice on his right, "Hey, champ, how's your day going?" and gently jabbed at him with his right fist.

The boy looked at him and giggled as Juanita's right arm lowered a plate in front of Daniel and her left arm a plate in front of Candace. As she scurried back to the kitchen, Daniel sniffed up the aroma and looked to his left, and asked, "How about you, princess?" The two-year-old also giggled and exuberantly pounded her fists on the table and kicked her feet from her booster seat.

"*Woah!*" he exclaimed, leaning back away from her. This ignited an equal response from Justice, who also began pounding his fists and kicking his feet under the table. Daniel looked back over at him and said, "*Woah!*" and tilted back the other way away from Justice. This incited an increased frenzy as the two competed with each other to make more noise and commotion than the other.

"Woah, woah," mimicked Juanita as she returned to the

table with two more plates for the children. She hovered near Justice, waiting for him to stop pounding his fists so she could deposit his plate in front of him. He looked up at the plate and parted his hands to make room for it. Juanita leaned in toward Grace, and she followed suit. They both looked at their food for a moment and then instinctively back to their father. He looked at Justice and then at Grace, picking up on his cue, and then across to Candace, who smiled back at him in anticipation. He bowed his head and closed his eyes, and the family followed his lead.

"Thank You, Looord," he began dramatically, "for this fooood." Both of the kids giggled. "Silence!" he demanded with a feigned scowl. The giggling muffled. "Thank You, Loooord, for this foooood," he prayed before changing his tone, "for Juanita who made it, and all of us who are going to eat it. Yours is the kingdom and the power and the glory forever, Amen!" He opened his eyes and looked around the table, "Let's eat! Man, this smells good, Juanita; thank you, thank you, thank you."

"You're very welcome," she responded gratefully before heading back for their drinks.

While the kids dug into their food, Candace surveyed her plate and wondered, *Why do we eat leftovers in this house?* but she held her tongue.

Noticing the slight scowl, Daniel asked, "What's up, honey?"

She snapped her head up and smiled, "Oh, nothing." She knew if she commented about the leftovers, she would get a very cheery response about how the leftovers were too good to waste, which, judging by the smell, was true. Juanita was very good at making a leftover gourmet meal into another, often *different*, gourmet meal. Nevertheless, *With that much money, why should they ever eat leftovers?* she thought.

"What did you do today, honey?" he continued.

She hesitated for a moment to muster enough courage to start a debate. "I was listening to a pastor talking about grace today."

Grace perked up and looked at her mom.

"Oh, yeah, what did he say?" Daniel asked, hoping to get a fresh revelation of some aspect of grace.

Candace continued, "He was saying that because of the grace of God, everyone in the world will go to heaven, because Jesus died for the whole world, and therefore the whole world will be saved, and that grace was like a filter for our sins so that God doesn't see them and therefore they are no longer an issue." She knew that wasn't going to go over well and calmly braced for his response.

Daniel, disappointed by the dis-revelation and eager to correct the error, responded, "Unfortunately, a lot of people believe that, but it's not what the Bible teaches. You can't just pick and choose what you want to believe. People do that to justify sin in their life, and preachers say that to pacify their people so they can keep their job, but it doesn't work that way with God. Titus tells us that grace teaches us to *deny* worldly lusts and to live *soberly* and *righteously* in this present world." (Titus 2:11–12.) Daniel stabbed a morsel of food and inserted it into his mouth. Grace had turned to look at him when she heard her name and continued looking back and forth as she heard her name repeated.

Candace took her cue and swallowed her food. "But doesn't that make sense, that if Jesus died for all, then all will be saved? How could Jesus die for everyone and everyone not be saved?"

"Because it depends on our response." He stabbed another bite and gestured with it as he spoke. "Yes, grace brings us salvation, but it also brings righteousness and empowers us to live righteously. That's what it says in Romans chapter five."

"Romans chapter five," she affirmed earnestly. "I remember that he said that the Bible says that where there is a lot of sin, there is even more grace. So that God's grace is greater than the sin, so God doesn't see the sin, so that however much sin someone has, there is even more grace. So, if a person sins a lot, there is even more grace to cover up the sin. That's how he said it works. So, however much a person sins, it doesn't even matter."

Hosea looked up, lifted his hands, and, despite the food in his mouth, pleaded toward heaven in frustration, "Oh, God, how can they do this to Your Word and take this out of context? Does anyone read the Bible to check what these people say? Do they train the people to not read Your Word, so they will believe whatever they say?" Everyone looked up at the ceiling with him as he vented his prayer. He lowered his hands and looked back at Candace, calming himself. "Grace is indeed greater and more abundant than sin, but it is not a covering grace; it's not a cover-up story. It's a cleansing and empowering grace. It teaches us and empowers us to live righteously and to do all the works of God that He has called us to do. We were created for good works in Christ." (Ephesians 2:10.)

His prayer and passion were a little overwhelming for everyone, so they all just looked at him for a moment while he chewed his food. He swallowed and started again, "Grace is the power of God to live righteously. If we abuse that grace, it will be worse for us in hell than if we never had any grace at all. The Bible says in Hebrews chapter ten that if we despise the grace of God through sin, we trample the blood of Jesus that saved us and that God will judge His people. It is true that God loves everyone, but He will not tolerate the plagues of sin in His people. Jesus came to deliver people from sin, not to save them so they can continue in sin, God forbid!" (Romans 6:1.)

There was an air of finality as he finished speaking that no one dared to challenge, and no one wanted to move either. As they all sat frozen in place, he gently stabbed at his food again, and since he wanted to restore the positive atmosphere, he turned to his baby girl and cheerfully stated, "And that is why we have Grace here."

She brightened up and smiled back at him.

He continued with increasing enthusiasm, "And she is such an awesome girl!"

She bounced lightly in her chair as her feet kicked underneath.

"And she's going to teach the world the true meaning of Grace!"

She escalated to giggling and laughing as Justice also started giggling, and Candace and Juanita exhaled in relief.

"Okay, now," he said jovially, "let's get back to dinner."

CHAPTER 17—THE FLESH DEBATE

As Candace looked for more reasons to justify her plight for freedom, she became more secretive in her research. She knew that the people and messages she was listening to would cause concern in Juanita and Daniel, so she found subtle ways to hide while she listened. She would put the kids down for a nap and close herself in her room with her phone and search out messages that could support where her heart was going, or, when Juanita was out shopping or taking some time off, she could watch and listen openly in the house. She began familiarizing herself with various people, channels, and programs that provided fodder for the fire of dissent, and she saturated herself with their words and themes. Her ears would tingle as she found sermons that supported her impending insurrection, the phone pulsing close to her craving ear. As she meditated on those words, over time, she would become emboldened to confront Daniel with her new findings.

One Saturday morning at the breakfast table, she tried him again. The kids had vacated the table, and the two were drinking tea and chatting about plans for the day when Candace decided to test him but with a softer approach than her last attempt. During a lazy pause in the conversation, she said in a curious manner, "I heard some people talking about the flesh this week; what is that all about?"

Daniel responded dismissively, "Well, it depends on who you're talking to, but most of the time, people are talking about their *flesh* as if that's the reason they can't stay away from sin, because the flesh, in other words, the power of sin, that is in them, forces them to sin against their will, like, 'The devil made me do it.'"

"Right," she agreed before testing him. "They were referring to Romans chapter seven, where Paul says that the sin that dwells in him forces him to sin against his will. So, if the great apostle Paul has to sin, what about the rest of us? We're not as good as Paul. If he had to sin, how can we resist?"

Daniel stared at Candace for a moment contemplating, "Let me tell you a story," he offered.

"Okay," she agreed.

"When I was a kid, my cousin and I had a paper route together. We loaded up our bicycles with bags of newspapers with rubber bands holding them together and threw them on peoples' porches every day before sunrise before we went to school. When it rained, we put the papers in plastic bags, and one of our parents would load them in the car, and we would throw them out the car window in the rain. And sometimes, my uncle would take us for doughnuts afterward which was really cool; yeah, the car would get a mind of its own and take us to the doughnut place against my uncle's will, and he would buy us each a doughnut."

"That sounds like fun," she interjected.

"Yeah, right," he agreed sarcastically. "The doughnuts were fun, but the rain was not," he explained while wiggling his fingers over his head to signify rain. Candace smiled back. "So, our paper route was about five or ten blocks around our house, and every month, we went out and collected the money from our customers. We bought the papers from the newspaper company and sold them and delivered them to our customers for a profit according to what the newspaper said we should charge, and some of our customers would give us tips and candy bars, etcetera. So, one day my cousin and I were walking down this driveway to two of our customers' houses. The houses were back off the street, and this driveway sloped down to their houses and split at the bottom with a house on each side. Are you with me?"

"Yes, a long sloping driveway down to two houses at the bottom," she affirmed.

"Right, so my cousin and I are walking down the driveway, and we're veering off to the house on the right when we hear this low growl from under this juniper tree," he continued with his voice fluctuating to create intrigue.

"Uh oh, a dog!" she warned.

"Right, so we freeze in our tracks trying to see where this growl is coming from, but the branches on this tree go all the way to the ground, so we can't see anything. We're about ten feet from this juniper tree when this German shepherd comes charging out of this tree at my cousin and me. We turn around and run up the driveway, and the dog is inches away from my cousin's heel when *yank!* he comes to the end of his chain."

"Ohhhh!"

"Yeah! So, we stopped running when the dog stopped, but our hearts were pounding, we were huffing and puffing, we were scared out of our minds, we were almost crying, and then we just started laughing, and the dog kept barking like crazy at us. After a few minutes, no one came out, and we couldn't get to the door, so we just left and went to the next house."

"Ha ha ha, that's funny."

"Yeah, I'll never forget that!" Daniel paused and stared off into the distance, reminiscing.

After an awkward moment of silence, Candace asked, "So what does that have to do with the flesh?"

Daniel looked back over at her, "That story has nothing to do with the flesh, but the way I *told* the story has everything to do with understanding the flesh. Because when I told the story, I used the historical present tense."

"The historical present tense?" she asked quizzically.

"Yes, the historical present tense. We use it all the time when we're telling stories like this. This is how it works.

You set the stage by establishing a point of time in the past like, 'When I was a kid, and I had a paper route,' and then once the scene is set, it becomes very natural to speak in the present tense as you're living out the story just like I did, 'And then this dog comes charging out of this tree.' So, we're telling the story like it's in real-time—like we're living it out right there—and it makes perfect sense."

Candace looked at him blankly.

"Right, so you don't know what this is because they don't teach it in school anymore, and if you used it writing a paper, then the teacher marked up your paper with a red pen telling you not to change tense. But you wrote it like that because you speak it like that. But we all used to write like that in America until about 1895 when someone wrote a grammar book stating that it was no longer proper to use the historical present tense when writing English. So, over a hundred years later, nobody knows what it is unless they are a linguist, which I'm not, but I learned about it by studying the Bible. I never even heard the term all the way through high school until I was in a linguistics class in college."

Candace continued looking at him blankly.

"I think that the historical present tense is used over fifty times in the Bible. Like when Jairus comes to Jesus to heal his daughter, and when Jesus goes to the mount of transfiguration with the three disciples, and a bunch of those other stories. So, if you're reading the older Bible translations, it's translated into the present tense like the original Greek, but in the newer translations, they change it to the past tense, so it's easier for today's readers." He paused to see if she was understanding. "So, when you see Paul writing in the present tense about his experience under the law, you think he's writing about his current experience, but he's not currently under the law—he's living in grace, do you see that? How many times does he say *law* there at the end of Romans chapter seven? Maybe fourteen or something. But he's not living under the law at that time; he's under grace, so why doesn't he say, I have this *grace* working in my body? Grace has this power over me. Why? Because I've got this dog chasing me up the driveway with his teeth inches from my ankles. He's talking about a past event in the present tense—like he's reliving it. He's talking about...he's making a general statement about life under the law before someone gets born again of the spirit. That guy that died in Romans chapter six did not resurrect in Romans chapter seven and then died again in Romans chapter eight. Then what do we say about Enoch and Job? And Zachariah and Elizabeth right there in Luke chapter one? God says they were blameless. What it comes down to is people looking for an excuse to sin. They're not interested in 'perfecting holiness in the fear of God' (2 Corinthians 7:1), so they can get closer to God; they just want an excuse to sin. They want to pretend that they can go to heaven and have their sin too. It doesn't work like that. They should be focused on walking in the Spirit instead of seeing how much they can live in the flesh; how much they can *get away with* living in the flesh. They don't get away with anything."

By the time he finished, Candace was catatonic. She heard everything he said, but that blank look on her face told him that it didn't make sense. Nothing she had learned to prepare her defense seemed like it would work now. This inability to refute put her in a stupor. Seeing her confusion, Daniel gave her an assignment, "This is what I want you to do; just listen to people's conversations. When I was in a writing class in college, my professor gave us the assignment to go to a coffee shop and listen in on people's conversations and use something we heard to write a story. So do that, just listen to people's conversations and *how* they tell stories from their past, just pay attention to *how* they tell their stories, and you'll see what I'm talking about."

"Okay," she said reluctantly, pondering the ethics of eves dropping on peoples' conversations.

Daniel reached out and hooked his arm around her neck and kissed her on the ear.

"Ouch," she cried out half-heartedly. "That was loud!" He kissed her again on the cheek.

Over the next few days, as Candace tried to make sense of what Daniel had been talking about, she listened to conversations, interviews, and people telling their stories and found that what he was saying was true about the way people merge tenses in storytelling past events. As the storytellers became more animated in relating their recollections, the more they spoke in the present tense.

She read about the people he referred to in the Bible, and she read the chapters in Romans, and it started making sense. But eventually, it came down to the fact that she just didn't care. She was going to do what she wanted to do no matter what Daniel, the Bible, God, or anyone else thought she should do.

CHAPTER 18—WHERE ARE THOSE PAPERS?

The increasing amount of Candace's questions and subtle emotional distancing brought uneasiness to Hosea. He was feeling more and more like something was wrong, but he didn't know exactly what. Although daily life seemed good in his home, he felt Candace slowly drifting away from him, and he was looking to God for answers. There was no clear response from heaven like he received in so many other matters, just a dull, mild heartache increasing from day to day. He wanted a tangible answer, a clear direction, a concise course of action, but all he could feel about any question concerning Candace was a somber, persistent pain.

He began questioning his effectiveness as a husband and a father. Was he doing everything he should be doing? Was he treating her right? Was he not properly teaching her how to pursue God, to seek intimacy with Him? He had taught her to read the Bible and pray, and they prayed for many things together, and he knew that she was reading her Bible often. He talked to her but couldn't seem to get past something there that was slowly separating them. He felt unable to penetrate that ambiguous *something* coming between them. He felt inept at reaching into her heart and finding that thing that was creating a wedge between them so he could take hold of it and yank it out. He felt there was some sinister multi-tentacled thing wrapping itself around her heart and tightening its grip with each passing moment, but no matter how he tried to reach in to grab it, he could not get his hand on it. He felt as if he were reaching in and, anticipating his movement, it moved away as he tried to take hold of it. He could feel but not see it, but *it* could see and feel him. He had an unfamiliar sense of helplessness to free her.

Examining himself, Hosea knew that he had never pushed her away at any time nor made her feel excluded. Sometimes she would feel awkward, not knowing or understanding why he did certain things or maintained certain rules, but as far as he could tell, he always recognized that and reached out to her and explained his reasoning, and once she understood, she readily accepted and embraced it; she never felt excluded for more than a moment. As far as mothering went, she always had help. He helped when he was home, but Juanita was almost always there. When she left, and Candace got overwhelmed, it never got really bad because Candace knew that Juanita would never be gone for more than a day or two, and she would get a reprieve. She embraced motherhood completely and rose to every challenge, learned quickly, and grew with every new test. Because of this, their kids were very happy. Daniel and Candace went out on a date at least once a week by themselves in the Ferrari and spent lots of time together as a family. He was also good at surprising her with little gifts and favors and other chivalrous romantic acts of endearment. He also looked to outside sources for guidance; books, teaching, preaching, and talking to married friends, but he wasn't finding a solution to his problem.

One day, he went to Los Angeles for a board meeting. One of the corporations of which he was a minor partner held a board meeting a couple of hours' drive away. Another investor, Bernie, drove him there. As they drove, Candace was at home thinking about the papers she had signed on that first day at the diner; where were they? She knew Daniel had to have put them somewhere, most likely in his study, but she wasn't brave enough to ask to see them. She knew his study superficially, the files and the bookcases, but she never looked for books on her own, and she had never been in the files. Most of the organizing was pretty logical, but she knew he had secret hiding places for personal things because he pulled something off a shelf one day for a friend when she was in there. On this morning, she played with the kids and spent some time with Juanita in the kitchen, but her mind was on those papers, which she knew were in the study. She had a feeling that the contract was hidden up there in the books.

Juanita liked to teach the kids Spanish. Mostly she just

jabbered at them for about twenty minutes, talking about whatever was on her mind, and occasionally found an object that she would teach them the name of, and they would repeat it a few times, and then it became a word they referred to from that time forward; like "*gato*" for *cat*, or "*silla*" for *chair*, or "*dígame*" for *tell me*. Justice could repeat most of the words, and Grace struggled a bit, but it was all fun because Juanita made it fun. They liked it when Juanita rolled the "R's" in words like "*perro*" and did Spanish alliterations and rhymes. She also looked for words that there was no way they could pronounce, which had both a humorous and entrancing effect on them. She usually did these lessons as it got close to lunchtime and would leave them practicing the new words while she prepared their food, but she could break into a Spanish babble at any moment if she wanted to get their attention in a positive way. So, when the kids started getting bored with their crayons that morning and a little grouchy, it was no surprise when Juanita started talking about her two friends, the "*perrrrrro*" and the "*torrrrro*," and started helping them put the crayons away. "*Ayúdame!*" she sweetly insisted as she motioned them to pick up the crayons, but they couldn't listen to Spanish and cleanup at the same time very well, so she paused the story until they got everything picked up. Anticipating a fun story, they quickly rounded up the crayons into their container and put their art off to the side to show daddy when he got home. Candace saw her opportunity and snuck out of the room toward the study.

Daniel kept the study locked when he wasn't in there, but Candace and Juanita had keys. She quickly unlocked and opened the door, and upon entering, she surveyed the expansive bookshelf. After a moment, she forced herself to look through the files first, in case she was wrong, and besides, she didn't want to search that massive bookshelf. She opened the top drawer and thumbed through the files looking for something that might be a label for the document. Her fingers danced through the tabs quickly, with her eyes tracking from side to side. She closed the top drawer and opened the next one, repeating the exercise. She raced through the tabs with little expectation of finding anything before slamming the drawer and turning back toward the wall of books. The study reminded her of Batman's mansion, and she envisioned Alfred working from the lair. The ornate dark cherrywood shelves rose to well overhead, and there was a sliding ladder to access the higher books. She remembered where he had pulled out the hidden document some months earlier and decided to start her search there. She walked to the wall and slid the ladder to where she thought he had retrieved the document. Mimicking his actions from memory, she ascended two steps as he had and started fingering through the books looking for any clue that might reveal where her document was hidden.

In Los Angeles, Daniel was sitting at the south end of a long rectangular table with twenty-one other investors, officers, attorneys, and accountants seated with him— all dressed in fine dark business suits. At the north end, there was a dry erase board that covered almost the entire wall. On the left part of the wall were well-organized charts, statistics, graphs, and projections. On the right were the semi-structured, handwritten notes from their brainstorming—plans, concerns, possibilities, and more projections. At the top center was a framed picture with a stylized rendition of a Franciscan monk imitating the famous Rodin statue, "The Thinker." *InvestorMonk* was one of Daniel's second-tier investments, he didn't own it, and he didn't need it, but it did provide connections in other important areas where he had interests. He invested time in the business, but more importantly, the meetings gave him an audience with important investment leaders he otherwise might not see. After the meetings, he met with these investors to keep a pulse on other markets that could impact his other investments. After taking a sip of his tea, Daniel placed his cup on the table and went into a vision. In the vision, he could see Candace thumbing through his books in real-time; he knew what she was looking for and why she wanted it. After a few seconds, she disappeared, and he was back in the meeting but very distracted. He turned toward the whiteboard staring blankly ahead. His prayers were answered, but he didn't like the answer. It was highly disrespectful to leave during the meeting, but impulsively, he pushed his chair back, softly said to Bernie, "Excuse me, I'll be back in a minute," and moved to the door a few feet away. Several heads turned as the door opened and closed, but the speaker continued. Daniel stepped down the hall, putting his ear to each door to find an empty room, the fourth room was vacant, and he stepped inside. He pulled out his phone and dialed his home office number.

The first ring startled Candace on the ladder; she gasped and jerked her head to see the ringing phone on the desk. She had *never* heard that phone ring, and she wondered for a moment who could be calling. She continued looking back across the rows of books. The phone rang five times before the message came on the speaker, "Hello, this is Daniel's private line, please leave a message, and I'll get back to you when I return to my study." The machine beeped, "Hello, Candace," his voice sounded out into the room. Her head jerked again to look at the phone with wide eyes and an open mouth. "Is everything okay? I can help you with whatever you're looking for when I get home." Daniel paused. Candace knew she was busted! How did he know? She looked around the room for cameras. Then she remembered Juanita's words, "Just tell him the truth; he knows it already." Her heart was pounding; she didn't dare answer the phone. His voice came back on, "I'm not sure what's going to happen here in Los Angeles, but I'll probably be home after dinner. Bye." He touched the screen to end the call and looked up at the ceiling, and vented his frustration in a muffled shout, "That was so stupid!" He looked down at his hand, which was shaking lightly. He looked straight ahead and took a slow deep breath, exhaled, and reached for the doorknob.

Candace clung to the ladder. Her brows furled, her eyes squinted, she clenched her teeth and tightened her lips. "Damn it!"

Daniel quietly slipped back into the room and found his seat as the speaker wrapped up his segment of the meeting, "So, I think that summarizes our agenda for the next quarter," he concluded. "I saw Daniel slip out of the room for a couple of minutes, so I just wanted to check if he had any questions before we move on."

As most of the crowd looked in his direction, but a few continued writing notes, Daniel looked up toward the speaker and again went into a vision. In a flash, he saw a series of notes and documents and airline tickets and heard conversations and understood a scheme of embezzlement. "Please forgive me for stepping out for a moment, but it sounds like everything is going in the right direction, and nothing sounds different from the information I had before coming here, but there is an urgent matter I think we need to address immediately." He turned to a blank page in his notebook, picked up his pen, and began writing down key information as he spoke. "Someone needs to look into why our accountant, Michael Reed, has purchased two one-way tickets on flight 147 to Singapore for Tuesday of this coming week with a certain Miss Sandra Turner, why he has made two five thousand dollar transfers from our company account into account number 000947832 at the bank of Singapore and then put almost nine thousand of that into the bank of commerce in Malaysia account number 0000427849, what he intends to do with that money besides buying airline tickets to Singapore and Malaysia and what he intends to do with the other *thirteen million* dollars he plans to transfer from our accounts on Tuesday morning before his flight. I believe someone can find all the appropriate documents in a brown leather folder on Miss Turner's kitchen table in apartment 247 at the whispering pines apartments on, *you guessed it*, pine street, right here in Los Angeles." He finished writing, tore off the sheet of paper, and passed it north up the table. "I recommend someone go to that apartment before Michael can reach her and inform her that we know what's going on and collect that attaché because she's there now working from home." All eyes turned to the frozen accountant seated a few people north of Daniel, on the same side of the table, as Daniel trailed off muttering, "I wonder if *Misses Reed* has ever met *Miss Turner?*"

The woman seated next to Michael, who had just lost control of his bladder, reached over to his phone and slid it over to the man on her other side.

CHAPTER 19—FOREIGN TRAGEDY

One weekday evening, Daniel failed to make it to the dinner table on time. It was one of those rare events when Juanita was a little overwhelmed and a little bit behind schedule, so when her Daniel-dinner alarm sounded, she could hear Candace in the dining room getting the kids seated at the table and solicited her help. "Candace?" came the call from the kitchen. "Are you out there?"

"Yes, I am," Candace called back as she situated Grace in her seat.

"Can you help me, please?" came the plea from the kitchen.

"Yes, I'm coming," she called back as she spun away from Grace's chair toward the kitchen. She came through the swinging doors as the slightly disheveled Juanita pulled a flat pan from the oven. "What can I do for you?"

"I haven't seen Daniel since this morning, and I need to take care of this food just now. I believe he's still up in his office. Can you go get him?" she petitioned as she blew a wild lock of hair from her face.

It looked like Juanita was having a rough time at that moment and that a trip up to the study was the better option, so Candace agreed to the task. "Okay, I'll be right back," and she headed back out the doors. "You two stay right there," she said to the little diners fussing at each other at the table. "I'll be right back…with Daddy."

"Yaaay," they chorused as she passed by toward the study.

She brushed off the nagging tension that had developed in her toward him over the last few months as she passed through the house, climbed the stairs, arrived at the door, and knocked, "Daniel, are you in there? It's time for dinner…Daniel?" She paused for a moment with her ear to the door before opening it and was surprised to see Daniel sprawled out on the floor on his belly with his face in the short red lava carpet covered by his hands. "Daniel, are you okay?" she asked while standing over him. She was a little annoyed that she had to come to get him, and now he was lying on the floor, sleeping?

To him, her faint voice sounded like it was coming from the far end of a long tunnel, echoing lightly as it traveled. The second time it was louder. The third time it was still louder, and he felt her hand on his back, and he was startled by the touch because the voice still sounded distant. He shuttered from the surprise of her touch before moaning through his hands, "What?"

"It's time for dinner. Are you awake?" she said while crouching with her hand on his back.

"I'm not hungry," he moaned.

"What's the matter?" she inquired, a little irritated. "Were you sleeping on the floor?" She didn't care, really, but she did feel she needed an explanation for Juanita and the kids.

Her voice was close to him now and out of the tunnel, and Hosea could still feel her hand on his back and felt he needed to talk to her because she was there asking. He began lightly rolling side to side, bringing his numb body back to life. As he struggled to get to a sitting position, she rose to her feet and watched him. He propped himself up on one arm. There was a big wet spot on the carpet where his face had been, and his face was red, and his eyes swollen. With the other arm, he reached for a handkerchief on the floor and wiped his face.

Candace did not know why he was like this, but he seemed very pitiful to her at that moment. She despised his having been on the floor, apparently crying...for what reason? He seemed like such a child. She asked him again indignantly, "What's the matter?"

After a long minute of composing himself, he started speaking weakly, "We had an orphanage in Africa and a church." He got off his arm and leaned forward, curling over his knees. "My friend David and me. He moved there, and I helped him build his church there." He used both hands to cover his face with the handkerchief and sobbed into it, stuttering, "A-a-and they burned it down." He sobbed uncontrollably for a moment before he could speak again, "He was my friend for a long time; we used to do a lot of stuff together. Then he started talking about Africa. He wanted to go there and feed the orphans, so he sold everything he had and went there, and I've been helping him." He sobbed for another moment gasping for breaths. "They put them all inside: him, the children, whatever people they could find nearby, in the two buildings, and they burned them down." He was convulsing and crying as he curled up tighter into a ball and rolled back over onto the floor, wailing loudly.

Candace was crying now. She had seen a lot of terrible things in her life but had never seen such a raw display of brokenness and pain, certainly not from a man and not from such a strong man like Hosea. She wiped a tear from each cheek and rushed out the door pulling it closed behind her, and pressed her forehead against her arm on the wall near the door.

She faintly heard Justice calling from the dining room across the house, "Mommy, where are you? Where's Daddy?"

She could still hear Hosea crying behind the door and envisioned him curled up like a ball writhing on the floor. She imagined the horror of little children screaming in the buildings as they set them on fire and were engulfed in flames. She shoved herself off the wall and pushed the horror out of her mind before confirming her resolve with a strong whisper, "I'm not going to let this stop me."

CHAPTER 20—THE JEWEL

Somewhere in the night, Hosea set his phone alarm so he could make an 11 a.m. appointment downtown. The alarm sounded as he lay on his study couch; he opened his eyes and hit the snooze button on the phone lying next to him. He had a terrible sleep and struggled to sit up on the couch. He rubbed his swollen eyes and massaged his face to get his eyelids to work and then blinked until the room started coming into focus. He saw the wet carpet and his handkerchiefs lying there. His heart still ached, and he wanted to stay right there and continue crying, but he knew he had an appointment to try to save a deal he had been working on for almost two years and was currently on the rocks, so he tried to motivate himself to move until the alarm sounded a second time. He turned it off and texted Juanita, "Can you make me some coffee, please?" By the time he reached his bathroom, she had texted him back, "Yes, I'll start it now," with a happy emoji. He showered, put on a gray business suit and a white shirt and an innocuous tie, and stared blankly in the mirror for a moment before braving the journey down to the kitchen. He was so emotionally spent that he hoped he would not encounter his wife or children and get out the door with just a brief word with Juanita.

When he got down to the kitchen, Juanita was waiting with his favorite coffee container for driving. As she handed it to him, she offered her condolences, trying not to cry, "Candace told me what happened. I'm so sorry. Are you okay?"

Struggling to keep his composure, he responded, "I'll be okay," tucked his coffee close, and reached out his other arm to give her a short hug. He desperately wanted so much more comfort than that, but he knew that Candace was not there for him, and he had to go. He pulled away from her and asked, "Are they in the learning room?"

"Yes, they are," she calmly affirmed.

"Okay, I'm taking my business car today," he declared somberly, referring to the same sedan he had picked up Candace on that first day. "I shouldn't be gone too long."

*****

Hosea took a deep breath as he stood outside the downtown San Diego high-rise office building and gazed toward his intended destination on the top floor. He stepped through the big glass double doors and then to the elevators not far behind that. He hit the call button for an elevator and stepped back to see which one would open first. As he stood there, he began thinking about the moment that Candace had come into his study the evening before. She saw him there weeping on the floor, heard what had happened, and walked out without a word of consolation. He could still see her expression for those few seconds that he looked at her, she was shocked, but there was no compassion in her eyes, not like Juanita this morning. That image was captured in his mind until the elevator sounded and brought him back to the lobby where he stood. The elevator opened, he stepped in, hit the button for the top floor, and turned to face the door. As the door closed, a hand reached in and stopped it; the doors retracted, and a shapely blonde woman with a form-fitting business dress and high heels stepped in next to him, glanced at the call button panel, and also turned to face the door before it closed. She was slightly winded from her effort to get to the closing elevator when she turned and said, "Hi, how are you doing?" as they started their ascent.

He turned toward her to respond, taking a half-step back. She looked so much like Candace that he thought it might be Katie. He couldn't entirely hide his intrigue as he tried to answer back as cordially as he could muster, "Hello, I'm doing fine. How are you?"

He had never seen her before, but she knew who he was and was relieved to see that he had selected the top floor but knew that she still had just a few moments to talk and hoped that no one else would join them for the ride up. "I'm doing good but slightly behind schedule this morning," she said cheerfully. Noticing a slight bag under his eyes, she continued, "You look a little bit tired."

Realizing that he had not effectively hidden how exhausted he felt, he blushed slightly. He wasn't sure how to respond and didn't know how to ask her if she were Katie; all he could say was "Uh," before she continued.

"You could probably use a vacation," she prompted with an easier comment for him to respond to as she glanced at the floor monitor over the door and then back at him.

"Yes, I'm sure I could," he agreed.

"Sometimes, you just need a little excitement during the week to chase those doldrums away," she proposed.

Hosea could only look at her as he thought, *What does she mean by that? This* must *be Katie. I should find out before she goes any further.*

"I have an office in this building," she continued, "and I can be a lot of fun during the workweek." She reached into her breast pocket and pulled out a card and handed it to him.

He took it from her hand, expecting to see some form of "Catherine" on it, but it didn't.

He peered over the card at her, "I'm sure you're quite the Jewel." The elevator stopped, and the door opened. Thinking she had achieved her goal, she winked at him. He looked toward the door and stepped out while she remained inside, and the door closed behind him.

He paused, looked at his watch—10:49 a.m.—and looked at the door in front of him and then back at the card. As he entered the front office, the receptionist was talking on the desk phone. He spotted the coffee maker and headed toward it. As he approached the table, the receptionist hung up and greeted him, "Good morning, Mr. Freeman. Mr. Simpson is expecting you."

Hosea dropped the business card in the trash can and, without realizing it, thought out loud, "A beautiful woman without discretion is like a jewel in a pig's nose." (Proverbs 11:22.)

"Excuse me?"

CHAPTER 21—THE DEPARTURE

A few days later, Candy stormed into the study with the contract rolled up in her hand. She threw it on the desk in front of Hosea, where it partially unfurled before him. The papers were curled on the edges and worn as if she had wrung them out many times since he had given them to her. "I want to go now, and I want my money," she demanded forcefully.

Hosea stared at the papers for a moment and slowly lifted his eyes to meet hers. He knew this moment was coming; this storm had been brewing for a while. He first felt its ominous rise that night in the bistro; nevertheless, he was both shocked and relieved when it arrived. He gazed numbly at her for a moment. His vacant, sullen, silent response only served to embolden her demand.

She was almost shouting, "I'm ready to go *now*, and I want my money!"

He knew he had to give her what she wanted, but he still thought the moment had arrived prematurely; he thought he would have three children with this woman.

He had to pay for two children, and she had fulfilled her obligation of waiting until they were weaned, but he was still one child short. He knew she would not contend for the children because of the contract and even more so because she wanted her freedom, and children would only get in her way. But he knew there was supposed to be one more child before she left. He began to tremble under the weight of his heartache, shock, and disbelief. Disbelief that this was really happening, he knew this day would come but now that it was here, its reality was far worse than he had imagined. Disbelief because she was leaving early, she couldn't leave with just having had two babies. He had written three potential babies into the premarital agreement because he knew God had moved him to do so, but she was leaving now, and there were only two, and still, he hoped that she would never leave. He felt disillusioned and disoriented.

"I'll give you your money," he almost whispered as he opened the center drawer and pulled out a checkbook and a pen. With all he could muster to keep his composure and still talk, chin quivering, voice trembling, he looked back up and asked her somberly, "Why do you want to go? You have everything a woman could want here. There's nothing you can't buy, we've traveled, we go out, we have fun, we have two beautiful children, and we *are* the one percent. This *is* the dream. Why do you want to go?"

Candy paused to look at him as he looked up into her eyes; he was broken. He was still barely able to function after losing his friend and the orphans in Africa. She started to soften as she looked down into his hurting eyes; they captured her and drew her in for a brief moment, she wanted to reach out to him, but as she felt herself melting, she quickly regained her resolve and slapped her hand on the papers. "I want my freedom," she declared, glaring down at him.

"Freedom?" he asked, visibly quaking. "Freedom? Was Stan freedom?" He had no idea why he said that, but it was out there now. Somehow, he knew where she was going.

Candace jerked back, and her eyes opened unnaturally large. Then, regaining her composure, she leaned in, squinting directly into his pleading eyes, shouting indignantly as he shuddered from the force, "I'm not going back to Stan. Now, give me my money!"

Hosea was shaking more now, first from the revelation and then from her shouting. He looked down and opened the checkbook. He could feel her hot breath on his head, pressuring him to write the check. He could smell her body and her perfume, and he yearned to hold her. His head swooned as he shakily scribbled out her name, the number, and the date, and he signed it. She could see that the number was right, and as he tore it from the book, she grabbed it from his hand, spun around, and marched through the door, slamming it behind her. Hosea pushed the chair away from the desk, turned around toward the couch, and lunged to the floor, sobbing uncontrollably.

CHAPTER 22—THE PARTY

Candy stepped out of her hot red Ferrari in her nearly matching red dress and handed the keys to the valet as the doorman watched from across the sidewalk. He was pushing away two men whom he had just denied entrance to clear the way for the approaching woman. Neither she nor the doorman for that exclusive club had ever seen each other, but they both instinctively knew that she belonged inside, so she made a seamless entrance with just a glance to the doorman. As he acknowledged her right to enter, she remembered how she could never have gotten into this club before and exulted in how easily she was entering now. The bland grey wall and black door at the sidewalk opened up to a hidden posh nightclub and vibrant party within. The pulsing music and colorful moving lights charged the dark room with an urgency to dance, drink, consume drugs, and do other unspeakable things.

Candy knew about this place before but could have never gotten in. You needed money to get in and a certain undefinable quality of character. She now had them both. One day out of prison, a trip to the *Exotic Exports* car dealer, a lot of shopping, and now she was here. For many years on the streets, she had wanted to come, and she was bubbling with excitement that she had finally arrived. In this place, she knew no one, but everyone was her friend. There was everything she wanted to indulge in, handsome men doting on her and freedom to do it all. Her excitement was contagious as she started mixing with the people at the first table she encountered. The night was on!

*****

At nearly two in the morning, Candy felt a hand gently shaking her by the shoulder and a man's voice beckoning her to wake up, "Ma'am, ma'am, it's time to go. We're closing up for the night; you need to go." One eyelid slowly lifted to see the dark, blurry figure, and then the other eye opened, and then the man started coming into focus. It was someone who worked there. As soon as he saw her eyes lock onto his, he knew she was awake enough for him to continue around the building. "It's time to go, ma'am," he repeated as she rose to a sitting position rubbing her eyes, and he moved on to the next room. She looked around, trying to remember where she was. The dark room had a few colored lights to help her get her bearings. She groped around with her hands until she found her new Louis Vuitton purse. She looked inside to find everything there except the cash she had spent, and now there were some drugs she had not come in with. She was in a private room by herself; apparently, the others had left her crashed on the couch. Had she passed out? Dizzy and disheveled, she tried to stroke her hair back into place with her fingers and straighten the wrinkles out of her dress as she rose to her feet. She stumbled to the door, opened it, and looked around the next large but dimly lit room and the people leaving for the night until she discerned the exit on the other side. She continued to regain composure as she made her way through the tables and chairs to the door, and by the time she got there, she felt halfway normal. A man opened the door as she approached, and she stepped out onto the sidewalk.

She recoiled at the city lights, which were much brighter than the club she had just exited. A man at the curb pointed at her as if he recognized her and was going for her car. She nodded back in affirmation. She sidestepped away from the door and stood near the wall surveying the street. It was all both new and familiar, the old streets with a new perspective. She fell into a blank stare before her car arrived and honked her back to attention. The man stepped out of the car and, once she was seated in the driver's seat, found some loose money in her purse and handed it to him, "Thank you, ma'am. Drive safely," he said, taking the money.

"Thank you," she replied as he closed the door on her.

Candy started down the road, not knowing where she was going. She just drove. Her mind had been fixated on buying her car, her clothes, and preparing for her night at the club; she had a pile of things she had bought in the passenger seat, but she hadn't given thought to where she would stay that night after the club. Instinctively, but without realizing it, she found herself driving toward the place where Hosea had picked her up several years ago. It wasn't far from the club, and as she mindlessly meandered through the city, the car took her to where she was destined to go.

It wasn't until she was a block away from the old neighborhood that she realized where she was. She gasped when she recognized the surroundings and then hesitated, but curiosity pushed her on. The streets were empty of people, and there was an eerie foreboding in the air. She saw the diner coming up on her left, the inside lights were off, but the security lights around the perimeter lit up the outside. She slowed down and looked to her right to see the old apartment where she had once lived. As she stared at the lifeless building, suddenly, a black cat chasing a rat came into the path of her car, leaped onto the hood, and ended up sprawled across the windshield. *"Eeeooow,"* it screeched. Candy jerked her head back at the sound. *"Aaaahhhh,"* she harmonized with the cat, slamming her foot on the gas and swerving off to the right where she had been looking. The cat leaped from the window, and a telephone pole loomed up in its place.

The next thing she knew, she was waking up behind the wheel of the sports car, the deflated airbag lying on top of her startled her, and she frantically fought to get it off, and she opened the door and fell out into the street on her hands and knees. She paused for a second and leaped to her feet. She moved to the front of the Ferrari, where it was smashed into the telephone pole. She gasped in horror, clasping her face with both hands and backing up into the empty street. She froze in the middle of the street and started to whimper. Her head was spinning, and she scuttled from the road to the curb behind the car, sat down, covered her face with her hands, leaned into her scraped-up knees, and began to cry.

She was only there for a minute before she felt a sharp pull on her hair, jerking her head back, and she heard a low, slow, familiar voice speaking straight into her ear. She recognized the cologne, the body odor, and the voice. A vision flashed through her mind of the last time she saw him marching across the street with that lethal glare. *It was Stan!* He started with a smooth melodic voice, "Well, look at what we have here, look what the cat dragged in. I knew I liked that cat for a good reason, and now I know what it was. He missed one rat and caught another." Candy's every muscle was locked into place; she couldn't move, she couldn't even breathe. Her eyes bulged, pointing almost straight up at the night sky. Stan had a large lock of her hair wrapped around his fist, which pressed against her skull; his whiskers scratched her ear as he spoke, "It looks like you got yourself a fancy call girl job. Is that what that man wanted you for? He just wanted one of my girls for a call girl, bought you that nice car, that nice dress, that sweet perfume. I'll bet he makes a lot of money off you with all that." Candy needed to exhale, but she couldn't. Her vision blurred. He started lifting her from the sidewalk by her hair as she remembered him doing so many times before; he was almost giggling, "Well, it looks like you got called to the right place. I haven't seen a call girl this pretty in a *long* time." The movement of rising to her feet pushed the air from her lungs, and she started breathing again; her eyes began darting around in a panic as her body followed the pull on her hair. Giddy with excitement, Stan continued, "I've got a place not too far from here where we can catch up some; we can't be too close when the police come to check on this car. I think you'll remember it when we get there. It's really quite romantic." Candy swooned as a wave of deep hopelessness swept over her, but Stan jerked her back in the direction he wanted her to go. Candy released a quiet, shrill, whimpering cry as he walked her away down the sidewalk, cackling.

CHAPTER 23—THE HOMECOMING

The next morning as the bedraggled Hosea ate his breakfast at the table, Justice asked him, "Daddy, where's Mommy?" He hesitated with a forkful of egg suspended at the portal of his mouth. As he started to answer, his cell phone rang where it lay on the table. He saw who it was and excused himself from the table. Stepping into the next room, he answered the phone, "Daniel speaking," and ascended the stairs to his study. As he closed the door behind him, he responded to the caller.

"So, she's okay, but she's recovering in the hospital," he summarized and paused for the response. "Can I come to get her?" Daniel asked eagerly. "Okay, I'll come down there, and we'll see what we can do."

Daniel was excited that he was getting Candace back in less than forty-eight hours. He didn't know anything that had happened during that time, but whatever it was, it put her in the hospital. He could only imagine. He was eager to find out, and he would readily forgive it all.

When Daniel came into her hospital room, Candace was

sitting up with her back against the raised adjustable bed. Her eyes were closed, and she had a cut on her forehead. He paused at the door after he closed it, gazing at her. The white sheets and gown against the light blue wall gave her an angelic appearance. Her disheveled hair and the cut on her head suggested that she had been injured in a fight. It was as if he were viewing an angel wounded in battle, and he was in charge of helping her recover. At that moment, all the heartache of the past months disappeared, and all was forgotten. He instantly became the doting nursemaid of this innocent wounded angel as if no offense had ever occurred.

He glided quietly to her bed and gently clasped her hand in his. After a moment, she started to nod her head back and forth slowly and open her eyes. A lone tear trailed down his face as her eyes fluttered open. She saw in his eyes the purest love and acceptance beyond what she could ever imagine a person could have. It so penetrated her soul that she could not possibly reject it or defend herself against it but, at the same time, had such a terrible conviction for the events of the last many hours that she burst into tears. Her tears only drew him closer, and he moved in to embrace her, and that gushing of love from him to her brought forth a torrent of tears and sobbing, and she began wailing openly. It was so loud that two of the nurses rushed in to see what was happening. There was such an overwhelming presence of tangible love in the room that they also burst into tears as they opened the door. Candace began crying out, "I'm so sorry, I'm so sorry, please forgive me, please forgive me!" Everyone's hearts felt as if they would burst, and they all began wailing uncontrollably so that the sound rang out through the hospital floor. Nurses, doctors, and visitors all began descending on the room and inexplicably bursting into tears as their hearts burst with love and joy. The news spread throughout the hospital, and eventually, the crying turned to laughing, and the laughing subsided to giggles, and it was late in the day before things settled back to normal. There was a noticeable improvement in every patient's health that day also, and a disproportionately high number of patients went home the next day.

After a few hours of crying and laughing, the couple made their way out of the hospital with rejuvenated spirits and a renewed relationship. They were still giggling on the drive home like a couple of newlyweds heading off to their honeymoon. They held hands intermittently and ogled each other at the traffic lights. Before long, they were back in the garage and paused for a moment to enjoy each other's presence before exiting the car. Candace leaned in close to Daniel and playfully locked her eyes onto his, reaching out to touch him, "Can we have another baby?" she asked, curling his hair in her fingers.

"Of course, we can," he responded spontaneously. "We can work on that today," he said with as much candor as he could muster. They both giggled and opened the car doors. They met at the front of the car and locked arms and leaned into each other to get through the door to the house. After just a few paces, two jubilant children charged into them, and the couple squatted to meet them, which turned into a group hug, and then they rolled over onto the floor laughing, rolling around, and flopping all over each other.

The next day, Candace had that vibrant glow that distinguishes expecting mothers. She never got sick and was unusually active throughout her pregnancy. She did gradually slow down, but it wasn't until a month from her due date that she noticeably exhibited the traits of a substantially pregnant woman under the burden of the soon-coming child.

There was never a word about Candy's lapse into the past. Daniel had never asked, and Candace didn't want to remember. It was treated as if it had never happened. Instead of guilt and shame, they leaped into a new paradigm of family joyfulness. Any details that surfaced about the totaled car, the hospital visit, and law enforcement inquiries were summarily dealt with, and their memories quickly dispensed into the sea of forgetfulness. The kids were too young to perceive or remember the growing hostilities before their mommy disappeared for a day, and the issue never arose again.

CHAPTER 24—THE GROCERY STORE

As Daniel and his family exited the local grocery store in the light, misty rain, a middle-aged couple from his church, Carl and Karen, were parking on the other side of the row across from them. Carl came to a stop in the selected slot, looked over the car parked in front of them, and saw the four approaching their car with a cart of groceries. The couple's curiosity caused them to pause and watch Hosea and Candace move toward their car.

"Carl, dear, isn't that Daniel there coming this way?" Karen asked inquisitively, peering across the lane through the water-spotted windshield.

"Yes, that looks like him; that looks like his car over there." He nodded toward the SUV parked with the rear end facing them several yards away, just across the lane.

"And who's that woman...? Is that his wife?" she continued.

"I think that's his wife," he answered hesitantly.

"He is married, right?" she asked incredulously. As they watched Hosea load the groceries into the car while

Candace loaded the baby in her seat and Justice made his own way to his seat behind the driver.

He answered with hesitation again, "Yeah, I heard he's married."

Sensing his hesitation, Karen felt that he was withholding information and continued more aggressively, "What does that mean? He's got a woman with him and a kid and a baby, and she looks pregnant. I've seen her at church with him. I never heard about a wedding, you would think he would marry some rich girl and have a big wedding, but I never heard anything about it. Did he run off to Las Vegas and get married? I haven't seen him at church as much."

Carl, hoping not to have to reveal some of the things he had heard, said, "Well," he cleared his throat, "Karen…"

They watched Hosea place bags into the back of the car as Candace, encumbered by her enlarged belly, put the baby in the car seat. Carl hoped to distract Karen from her questioning, and his curiosity caused him to linger as he also gawked at the attractive pregnant woman in wonder.

After a lengthy pause, his wife continued with a prying intonation, "Well, what?"

Looking back at his wife, he started awkwardly, intending to protect Hosea from an inquisition, "Well, he travels a lot, so he's not always around, and we miss some days too, and we probably go to a different service time also, that's why you haven't seen them. Men get busier when they start a family," he postulated.

She continued again suspiciously, "He used to be in *all* the services; where did he find that woman? There's something different about her." She glanced back at the car as Candace hurriedly tested the safety straps on the baby, closed the rear side door, and entered the front passenger door while Daniel finished loading the food bags. Carl also looked back at the car to avoid the conversation with his wife.

Karen looked back at him and continued with a concerned voice, "Well, what happened...? Did he *accidentally* get her pregnant, where did she come from, how does he know her?" she fished.

Carl, still hesitant to answer the questions, and wanting to avoid Karen's eyes, continued looking at Daniel.

Karen followed his lead and watched as Daniel closed the hatch and rolled the cart toward the corral in the store's direction. Then she looked at Carl and continued, "He was always such a center of attention with the things he said and all those people that got healed, the cancers and all that other stuff, Kate and Leo, and..." she stretched the name out for emphasis, "Sylllvia. What about that?" She continued reminiscing the familiar routine with an air of envy. "He would just kind of quietly step to the front, and it would get real quiet because everyone knew something was about to happen. He was such a meek man, and he talked so calmy. Then he would say someone was getting healed or prophesy something good thing was about to happen to someone, with everyone just hanging there, frozen, waiting to see what would happen. Then, by the time he finished, everyone would clap and be happy. Now (gesturing toward the car), he got this woman pregnant. What happened?"

Carl, with his hands on the steering wheel, dropped his head and gently collapsed forward in remorse.

Karen analyzed his brokenness momentarily before continuing her interrogation, "He was always so chummy with Pastor Charles, the pastor had so much respect for him, but since this woman showed up, they don't seem so friendly anymore." She paused for a moment, "Well, what happened?"

Seeing that it was futile to withhold information any longer, he slightly raised his head, looked at her sideways, and, resigning his vow of silence, solemnly confessed, "He married a prostitute."

The words hung in the air for an eternal sublime moment as she stared at him. In the background, Hosea, now humming a happy gospel song in the drizzle, returned to his car, disappearing as he entered the driver's door, and started the engine.

With both disbelief and the satisfaction that she had gotten to the bottom of the matter, Karen stuttered accusingly, "He-he-he what?"

Carl Lifted his head and looked straight forward as Hosea's car backed out and then drove past them, the passengers still unaware of the onlookers' presence. Carl found resolve and explained, "I heard that he married a prostitute, that he had her hidden in his house for months before they got married. That's all I heard. I haven't seen him much until now, maybe it's true, I don't know. I don't know what's true, and I don't know what else to say, but I don't think we should talk about it because I don't *really* know. I don't know if anyone *really* knows, and it doesn't seem plausible, but that's what I've heard."

She stared at him for a moment, gaping, as still as a department store mime, before looking back through the windshield at the empty space where Hosea's car once stood.

Carl stared for a moment also and then opened his door before looking back at the bewildered and now angry woman and, with a sigh, prodded her gently with an invitation, "Let's go get some food."

CHAPTER 25—MERCY

On a fine, sunny Saturday afternoon, DJ was born, which stands for Daniel Junior, his first name was Mercy, but before he was born, they were already calling him DJ. The birthing was a simple procedure. Candace's water broke shortly after breakfast; Daniel called Dr. Leafman, put their delivery bag for the hospital in the 4x4, and he drove Candace to the hospital. She was contracting sufficiently when they got there, so they took her straight to the delivery room; she pushed a few times, and out he came. She rested a bit in the hospital, and they were all doing so well that the doctor in charge sent them home before sundown. You could hardly ask for an easier delivery. Candace was a little disappointed that she didn't get to stay in the hospital longer, at least overnight, and get a little more professional pampering, but, at the same time, she didn't like hospitals, so she was even happier to get home.

Once they got home, the reality of having another baby sunk in quickly, especially for Candace. It was no major inconvenience when DJ was inside her belly, besides carrying the extra weight, but now that he was out, she had to care for him. He wasn't an especially difficult child, but there were late-night feedings, intermittent sleep times, diaper changes, and other such baby stuff. Daniel did what he could to help with their new baby, but he wasn't always there, and ultimately, the responsibility fell on Candace. There are many doting people wanting to admire the new baby, hold him, play with him, make silly faces, and other ways we entertain ourselves with the little bundles of joy, but when the need arises, we hand them back to Mommy, who feeds them, burps them, changes their stinky diapers, wakes up in the middle of the night, and provides all the other maintenance required to keep them at bay. The visitors just get to enjoy them for a moment and then hand them back. *Mommy* has to care for them.

There were also the other kids. Justice and Grace were feeling the squeeze for attention in the wake of the new competition, which always came first. His needs always came before theirs. Playing second fiddle to the new baby brother wasn't sitting comfortably with either of them, so little attitudes were flaring up more frequently and had to be corrected more often. It wasn't long before Candace began to weary with the project. She was a wealthy stay-at-home-mom with an amiable and industrious nanny to help her, an enviable arrangement that most mommies would dream of, but once again, she began yearning for freedom.

Candace's dream for freedom, however, was constantly

put into check with memories of her last escape attempt. Like a hailstorm interrupting a sunny day at the seashore, memories of her car smashed on the telephone pole would drive away all hopes of once again pursuing that elusive freedom that repeatedly consumed her thoughts. In less than twenty-four hours, she had bought and totaled her dream car and spent hours with Stan torturing her before he dumped her back out on the street, and as the memory returned, she had to stop it because she could not bear to remember Stan; she knew he was still out there, somewhere, and if she left again, he would find her.

Juanita would sometimes catch Candace grimacing and shaking her head for no apparent reason. "Are you okay, Candace?" she would ask with concern. Candace would quickly recover with an assuring affirmation that all was well. "Just a bad memory," she would say. That disastrous event, that totally botched, ill-conceived, incompetent attempt, served to prove her absolute ineptness to escape this dreadful enslavement she imagined herself as being confined to, chained to three fussing and needy children. The dreadful memories that haunted her from day to day wearied her mind and her soul.

After just a few months into her third baby, Candace was getting grumpy, short-tempered, and snappy. "Hey," she barked at Grace and Justice one day while they played. "Stop it!" she shouted with agitation while pushing them out of the room. It wasn't that they were doing something wrong but that she wanted to be somewhere else, doing something different. Her patience was short, and her temper sharp. Juanita was a neutralizing force for Candace's worsening distemper, but it seemed to her that this ship was heading into the rocks.

It was not so when Daniel was home. Daniel was always singing some happy song. Most of the time, they were his own spontaneous creations that just sprang forth from a happy heart. He had songs about his children, Candace, Juanita, friends and strangers, work projects, bugs, and just about everything else; he was a living musical in action. As soon as Daniel came through the door, the atmosphere changed; the baby stopped crying, the kids stopped fussing, and everyone got happy, even Candace; all those terrible thoughts and emotions would instantly vanish. Like the skilled young David playing his harp for the demonized King Saul, Daniel was the cure for any emotional malady in the home. Everyone in the house gravitated toward Dad as soon as he appeared, boisterous chatter erupted, and Justice and Grace clung to him like monkeys on a banana plant. One day in the kitchen after dinner, when the kids had been whisked off to the tub with Juanita, he burst into a robust, opera-like version of "Amazing Grace" that absolutely captivated the love-struck Candace, and he was unable to finish before she lassoed him with a dishtowel and rounded him up into the bedroom. Daniel's voice wasn't great, but it was good enough. That wasn't really what mattered anyway; it was the happy sound that counted. Daniel's joy was both magnetic and contagious. The grumpier Candace got, the happier Daniel seemed to be. He knew nothing of

Candace's deteriorating mental health because he never saw it, and Juanita had yet to tell him.

CHAPTER 26—A NEW WOMAN

One night when Daniel was out of town, DJ was up three times hungry or just crying. Just as Candace would fall off to sleep, his crying would erupt, and *up* she was again tending to her dependent infant. After the sun rose, she staggered from her bed to the breakfast table. Her eyelids wavered up and down, and she swayed slightly from side to side with a vacant stare while holding her coffee mug with both hands. It was a good thing she didn't have to go to work, and she was glad she had a nanny. She was too tired to get upset and too tired to do just about anything but sit and stare. She tended to DJ throughout the morning when he wasn't sleeping, and after lunch, she thought she could get a nap at the same time as the kids. So, after putting them in their beds, she meandered to the living room couch and laid down to sleep. She lay on the couch with her head supported comfortably by a pillow while looking into the fish tank. The fish swam peacefully in the tank as her eyelids slowly sunk down and closed.

As she fell off to sleep, she began to dream. She watched almost every challenging moment in her relationship with

Daniel and the kids. Her family had brought so much joy to her life, but this dream was void of any of those memories. She remembered her debates with Daniel, and she saw the challenges of motherhood and felt the burden of dependent children. First, there was Justice and the neediness he brought to her life, and then when Grace came along, she felt the burden double. They were crying, pulling on her, demanding her to help them. Then she held them both in each arm, and they got heavier and heavier. "Mommy, Mommy, Mommy," they cried, vying for attention. Then DJ appeared, crying in his crib, and she put the two down and picked him up. He was much lighter than the other two, and he became happy and giggly in her arms; the other two clung to her legs, clawing at each other and tugging on her skirt for her to pick them up. Suddenly she found herself in a ticket line at the airport. The people were moving in front of her, and she advanced forward behind them, holding the infant while Justice and Grace clutched each leg, and the line extended behind her. She reached the ticket counter, and a pretty, blonde lady with an airline uniform and hat, a big smile, and bright red lipstick politely asked, "Can I have your baby, please?"

"Excuse me?" the bewildered Candace responded.

"Can I have your baby, please?" she cheerfully repeated, batting her eyes.

"Why do you want my baby?" she questioned.

"For your ticket, of course," she continued undaunted.

"My ticket..." Candace paused. "To where?"

The ticket lady just smiled and looked up over her head. Candace followed her lead, and, looking up, she saw that instead of information boards with flights and times and destinations, there were backlit, stained-glass pictures of tropical paradises with beaches, waterfalls, coconut palms, butterflies, toucans, and macaws. She started turning to follow the pictures around the room, and they got larger and filled every space like a giant mosaic with oceans and coral reefs with sea turtles and brightly colored fishes. The vibrant fishes released from their canvases and were swimming playfully in the air around her, the children and airport had vanished, and she was reaching out to touch the fish as they scurried away from her reach. She recognized some of the fish from her tank, but there were many others. It seemed like they were swimming in water with her, but she was in the air in their midst. She was filled with wonder and amazement, watching the brightly colored schools of fish swimming gayly as one body, glimmering and flashing like sequin rainbows as they floated around her.

Suddenly, it all disappeared, and she was back at the counter looking at the airline ticket lady. "Can I have your baby, please?" she asked again with the same cheerful demeanor.

Candace's mouth was still hanging open from her sea life experience as she now gaped at the lady dumbfounded. She looked back up to see flights and schedules on the boards overhead and slowly looked down at the baby, who was still giggly, and then she looked back up at the lady.

"For your ticket to paradise," she expounded.

Candace jolted with revelation, and her eyes and mouth widened even more. She looked down at the baby again and quivered as she lifted him up to the ticket lady who reached out over the counter to take him. The woman politely took him from her arms and gently placed him to the side and then reached down for a ticket and handed it over to Candace, who took it from her, looked at it for a moment, and then looked back up at the ticket lady.

"You're free to go now," the woman concluded with the same buoyant grin.

Candace's eyes popped open, and she found herself lying on the couch. Her eyelids blinked rapidly as she sat up and drooped her legs over the edge, her hands propping her up on each side. She sat there, paralyzed with shock, pondering the dream. As she did, the tank came into focus, and she recognized some of the fish from her dream. A plan began formulating in her mind. This whole time she could only reflect on how she had failed on her first escape attempt, but she had another baby now, and once he was weaned, she would be free to go, and she would have money again, only half as much, but that would be quite enough to get her back out of that maternal prison. She still had money in the bank left from the first check, and she didn't need to spend any of it. She would get another check, and she wouldn't get a Ferrari this time. She would do things differently; she had learned her lesson. Next time she would be frugal. Candace had no true concept of frugality or long-term financial planning, but the illusion created by her afternoon dream made her think she did. The days of lamenting her past failure were over; she now had a plan for the future.

In the following days, Juanita quickly noticed the difference in Candace's attitude and behavior. The strange episodes of shaking her head and talking to herself ceased. She suddenly had all the patience needed to handle all of her children's needs without getting upset. Her parenting skills sprung forward several notches from that day forward. She juggled and met every child's need simultaneously without any fuss or complaining, which had a calming effect on them all. Juanita had been on the verge of discussing Candace's strange behavior with Daniel, but there was no need for that now, it was gone, and peace was back in the house when Daniel was not home.

Daniel had no idea that anything had ever been wrong since her return. He had always carried his own positive atmosphere with him wherever he went, and since that day at the hospital, it had only intensified. In his heart, he had accepted that the one tragic night back on the streets had cured Candace of any possibility of leaving again. This brought a deep assurance to his soul, which expressed itself through an unquenchable optimism and joy. The former underlying expectation and fear that Candace would return to the streets had completely vanished. He always looked forward to coming home, and when he got there, they all felt it in an almost magical way. He was like that man described in the Carpenters' song, "Close to You." He had no knowledge of the strange things that had previously transpired when he wasn't home and Candace's mental ticks, all he knew was what he brought with him because everyone naturally responded to his exuberant disposition. It was impossible for them to carry any animosity or emotional ills while he was present. Whatever song he was singing became their song, and if they couldn't keep up, they just hummed along.

Candace didn't carry the pure, joyful presence that Daniel had, but her newfound goal and optimistic determination that she would fulfill it made her a very enjoyable person to be around; she was fake but convincingly genuine at the same time. Fake in that she had no long-term intentions of staying with her family, and therefore, her daily devotion to her children, husband, and home was not real. Genuine in that she had a perfect plan, inspired by a dream, that she felt empowered to execute perfectly. Understanding that she had her ticket to paradise and freedom, she cherished, protected, and cared for that ticket to the utmost of her ability. That blissful display of devotion was perceived by those around her as a devotion to her family, to motherhood, to wifehood, and she was beautiful to look at—so it all played out perfectly. They responded to her enthusiastic positivity in like manner, and it seemed like she had the ideal family relationship which no storm of adversity could ever topple. Her children (although she did not perceive them as hers—she was merely their surrogate mother) were fun to play with and care for, and she *did* love them. She had the best job in the world. She reminded herself, "I get to nanny a billionaire's children for less than two years, and then I get a huge paycheck;" that was her perception, her personal secret. She was just there for the baby, *her ticket*, but her performance was well-sufficient for her doting children; they adored her for just being there. They never knew what had transpired that one dreadful night or her plans for the future.

Candy knew the details of the contract and dedicated herself to carrying them out perfectly. That wasn't so hard, but she had also learned from Juanita, the Bible, the church people, and the radio preachers the traits of a virtuous woman, homemaker, and mother; she put all of her efforts into being that woman. The fish tank was a constant reminder of her goals, and whenever she felt her energy and positivity waning, she would take a moment to watch the fish and rejuvenate herself by remembering the prize. The days quickly turned into months and a year, and in almost no time, DJ was two years old.

CHAPTER 27—THE BIRTHDAY SURPRISE

There was great joy on DJ's second birthday. Hosea had a grand celebration with fun, food, and festivities for the kids and classy, catered cuisine for the adults. He spared no expense in attracting parents, so they, in turn, would bring their children to the party. He knew the many things that vied for people's time and attention, and he determined to outdo them all for this grand event. He had jumpy houses, puppets, a ventriloquist, and other entertainers throughout his front yard and a colossal cake in the center of it all. He began sowing seeds of intrigue months before the event. Then he periodically added tantalizing little details, boosting curiosity and desire as the day approached. People who had made other plans changed their calendars as they began feeling a sense of loss if they, and their children, should miss out on such an event. They were not disappointed to the slightest degree.

People started showing up at 11 a.m., but the party officially began at high noon when a couple of gunslingers met on the front lawn. They started at opposite sides of the yard about ten minutes before twelve, hurling G-rated curses, insults, and accusations at one another, harnessing the unsuspecting crowd's attention with their loud, flamboyant speech. The cowboys paced around, trying to get a better position on each other on the spacious lawn. They circled back and forth, dispersing the people away from the firing line, which shifted as the cowboys both looked for cover and advantage over each other. People dashed around as the outlaws, seemingly oblivious to the bystanders, escalated the argument. Finally, at exactly noon, the arguing ceased, and six rounds were fired from all four guns, and both cowboys fell to the ground in a blaze of gunfire. They lay there on the ground for a long, extended moment, with gun smoke lingering in the air, the crowd mesmerized. A sense of wonder and confusion ruled the moment when suddenly, they both rose to their feet and, with great animation, shouted, *Happy birthday, DJ!* The two-year-old, who was watching from behind a puppet house, was captured on video with eyes bulging, lips drooling, frozen in place, while the whole crowd echoed, *Happy birthday, DJ!* And the party began.

Daniel had warned everyone not to be late for the grand start and had set the target arrival time for 11:30 a.m. Nevertheless, some of the fashionably late heard the shots and the shouts from down the street or not at all and had to hear about it for the rest of the day. That was all part of the fun. As the resurrected cowboys approached the birthday boy to say hello, the catered food came out, and the roar of excited chatter filled the estate. After about an hour of eating, various entertainers performed at intervals throughout the day, with breaks in between each show.

Later in the afternoon, all the excitement was too much for little DJ, and he cried for a few minutes and then fell asleep right there on the lawn. A few of his peers followed suit. The entertainment ceased for a while, and after almost an hour, he came back to life, and the next event went into action. Whenever the cowboys, who were mingling in the crowd, came across each other, there were threats of another gunfight, which never occurred, but it was one of the many things that kept the crowd on their toes and the excitement brimming.

About thirty minutes before sunset, the two candles were lit, the birthday song was sung, the flames were blown out, and the cake was served. As the sun neared the horizon, bubbly apple cider was dispersed throughout the party in clear plastic cups, and the happy dad closed the evening with a blessing for his look-alike son amidst the happy crowd, who toasted the child with a final cheer before dispersing into the night.

It took an hour for Daniel and Candace to say good night to their friends, corral the kids into the house, and hand the final cleanup off to Juanita and the security. They were tired but still wired with excitement. The kids got their baths, put to bed, and fell asleep instantaneously. When Daniel kissed his last child on the forehead, he went into his office to finish up some work that had been put off to prepare for the party.

Because Candace had never shown any dissatisfaction with the relationship since returning from the hospital, had never argued or debated, had never given any indication of her plans to leave, the moment she came back into Hosea's office with the curled-up contract in her hands was a complete surprise. Like the first time, he was working in his office, seated at his desk, facing the door, head down, working on a project. The door opened quietly. Candace entered, strolled to his desk, and triumphantly dropped the papers on the desk before him. With his head still bowed, Hosea glanced from his writing to the papers. He recognized them from before but had no idea why they had just fallen on the desk in front of him. He raised his head to look up at Candace's face and, in his innocent naïveté, sweetly asked her with a smile, "What's happening, Candace?"

In her madness, Candy, realizing from Hosea's complete absence of the slightest suspicion that she had any intention of leaving, even with the contract sitting right there before him as it had been almost three years earlier, paused for just a moment gloating in the absoluteness of her success in keeping her secret so perfectly hidden from him, until an involuntary giggle slipped up from the midst of her desperately wicked heart and emerged from her smiling lips in a short, tell-tale, burst, "Ee-he."

That little sound, carrying the very embodiment of betrayal from which it came, savagely pierced Hosea's tender heart and sent shock waves through his soul and a tremor throughout his body. His bowels weakened, his stomach seized, and the strength seeped from his body. As he slowly slumped down onto his desk, an almost imperceptible whimper escaped from his contracting diaphragm, "Aaaaooo." Like a dying man releasing his soul in his last breath, Hosea continued to lean forward until coming to rest there on the top of his desk.

Candy, reveling in the perfect execution of her flawless feat of deception, calmly stated, "I'm leaving *early* in the morning; I want my check before I go," she pivoted and stepped from the desk and back through the door, closing it silently behind her.

Hosea had no warning or expectation that Candy would be leaving again. There was no season of preparation, no incremental breakdown of communication, and no waning affection and care leading to the expectation of an imminent separation. He had no warnings like the first time. In a single unanticipated moment, his only earthly romantic love relationship came to a final and abrupt end. Waves of grief and horror swept over his seemingly lifeless body, and he began convulsing with sobs and groaning with the unbearable pain of heartache and separation. He eventually shook out of his chair and fell to the floor.

At that moment, Hosea had a taste of the pain that his eternal Father, Jesus, and the Holy Spirit must feel at the betrayal of His church, His bride, who has, through so many millions of people, now and over the centuries, betrayed Him through so many countless sins. Was God this broken over each one? Does His supernatural capacity to love have an equal capacity to hurt? It must. Is each offender so insensitive about the pain brought to the heart of their intensely loving God with every sin against Him?

In this darkest moment, Hosea felt that he was sharing in that pain, and there was no consolation for him there, just the deepest heartache he could possibly imagine. How his Father must ache over every lost soul.

At some point during the night, a check was written, signed, and placed on the desk. Just before dawn, as he lay lifeless on the floor, Hosea heard her slip in, take it from the desk and step out. For the second time, Candy was breaking the heart of a man who would lay down his own life for her without hesitation. For the last time, she was closing the door of that grand house behind her because this time, again, she planned to never return. She took nothing of his when she left but the clothes that she wore, a purse, and a check. In this ultimate deception, she had no concept of what she had left behind. He had no idea where she was going, but he knew it would not be paradise. Candy had left on DJ's second birthday, the exact date that she was obligated to stay under the contract until he was weaned: two years.

CHAPTER 28—WHEN IS MOMMY COMING HOME?

Hosea never made it to the breakfast table the next morning. Candy was gone and Juanita, not knowing what had happened, instinctively stepped in to take her place, feeding the kids. Hosea, immobile on his study floor, could not muster the strength to rise and certainly could not contain himself in the presence of his children. His heart was heaving inside him, and his stomach was twisted tight. He was locked in his office and rolling around sluggishly, crying and moaning.

The children were used to having breakfast with Juanita, so nothing seemed out of order to them. Sometimes Mommy fed them, sometimes Juanita, and sometimes both, so there was no perceptible change. Juanita figured Daniel and Candace were sleeping in after the big party and would let them do so for as long as they wanted. However, it was Sunday, so they should be on their way to church before too long.

The children were fed and cleaned up and dressed, and

it was almost time to go. Juanita looked at her watch and then went looking for Daniel and Candace. She found the bedroom door open and everything clean, but no one inside. It seemed strange because she hadn't heard a sound all morning, so she kept looking. Now she felt like she was in a horror movie as she timidly went from room to room, cautiously looking around each corner as she went and tapping lightly on every closed door before she opened it or passed to the next one. She was heading toward the library. When she reached the locked door, she tapped lightly and waited, then knocked louder, "Daniel, are you in there?" There was no sound. She knocked again, "Daniel, are you in there?" She waited again. She knew that sometimes he fell asleep there working. She closed her eyes and leaned her head on the door so she could hear anything inside. As soon as her forehead touched the door, it opened suddenly. She jerked her head up and gasped in surprise. There stood Hosea looking as sick as death, with the door open just enough to see his head.

He spoke in a hoarse, broken voice, "Juanita, Candace is gone. Can you take the children to church for me today?"

Terrified but recovering quickly, she thought, *Candace is gone. What does that mean?* She contemplated Hosea and his words for a moment and stuttered, "Sure, I can do that."

"Thank you," he gurgled and closed the door.

Juanita clutched her heart with one hand and released a deep breath. "Candace is gone," she whispered to herself and headed off to get the kids in the car. She hurried down the hall, knowing it was going to be a tight race to the church to get the kids there on time by herself. She found them all playing where she had left them. "Come on, kids, let's go. We're going to church without Mommy and Daddy this morning." She put her arm around DJ's chest from behind and lifted him up and away from his toys. She grabbed Grace by the hand and beckoned the eldest. "Come on, Justice, hurry, let's go. We don't want to be late." He fluttered for a moment with the block he was placing on his castle and then dropped it and went after them.

Juanita brought them across the house to the garage door and, as she opened it, declared, "We're going in the SUV." She released Grace and hit the button that opened the SUV garage door. Then she opened the car door where the baby car seat was and placed DJ in there and buckled him up. The other two found their way to their seats and buckled in, and Juanita tugged on the belts to test them. She got into the driver's seat and buckled herself in. She started the car, put it in reverse, and watched the screen as she backed out. When she got into the driveway, she hit the button to close the garage door, put the car in drive, and went toward the front gate. As she pulled up to the gate, she heard Grace say from the middle seat, "When is Mommy coming home?" Juanita hit the brake and froze, looking in the mirror at Grace.

CHAPTER 29—SURPRISE

After mourning Candy's estrangement for about six months, Hosea had come to believe that she would not be returning. All the evidence she left behind indicated that she had gone to a tropical island somewhere. There were a few paths he could have pursued to find her, but he chose not to do that. They had an agreement that he had written up based on what God had told him. She fulfilled her part and left with the money; that was her right. He knew all of this would happen in advance, but that didn't stop him from loving her, it didn't ease the heartache and the shame, and it didn't help their children. He couldn't ever tell them the whole story; he didn't think he could. He couldn't tell anyone the *whole* story. Pastor Charles knew, Dr. Leafman knew, and Juanita knew, but that was all.

He still missed her most in the mornings. He always woke up thinking about her, missing her, longing for her to be there next to him when he woke up, reaching out to touch her. At some point during the morning, eventually, business would push her out of his mind, and usually, by

223

lunchtime, she would be forgotten until the end of the business day. When he saw his children's faces, he would be reminded of her again. He saw her in all of them. Whatever drove her memories away during the day, they always came rushing back the moment he saw one of their children.

The weekends were the hardest because there was nothing to drive those memories away. Sometimes he would have some little business details to work out on Saturdays but nothing substantial enough to make her disappear from his mind. He spent the days with his children, so, all day long, he was seeing Candace: three of her. But he knew that it was worse for them; how could they ever have closure? One night after DJ's birthday party, Mommy just disappeared. That wound was always open in their hearts. There was a sense of disorientation that held them from that day forward. The mutual sense of abandonment that they shared was seen and felt every day and permeated every aspect of their lives. They would still look for their mother for direction and comfort but would never find her. Surely, eventually, they will get over that, won't they?

As they sat at the breakfast table that Saturday morning, Hosea was enjoying watching his three children as they ate; his three Candaces. They had just started eating the pancakes and turkey sausages when he sat down, and they didn't notice him admiring them. Justice and Grace were skillfully using their knives and forks, but DJ was just using his hands, dipping the sausages in syrup and putting them in his mouth, dripping syrup all the way. Juanita was gone for the weekend, so it would be all Hosea cleaning that up. It didn't bother him one bit; it was all part of the day's adventure. Daniel Jr. was alternating the sausages in each hand, dipping them in the syrup, and taking a bite and would need a full bath by the time breakfast was over. The syrup was fun like that for him; he got to eat it, play with it, and when he finished, someone would wash it all away. Justice and Grace enjoyed the syrup but were careful not to touch it with their fingers and were very diligent in keeping it off their faces. Mercy was not so; he fully embraced the sweet, sticky messiness, sometimes even rubbing it on his arms and face as he ate. He was sitting directly across the table from Hosea, with Justice on Hosea's right and Grace on his left.

Once the two sausages were gone, it was time for DJ to eat the pancakes. He took one silver dollar-sized cake in each hand and dipped them in the syrup and continued with the same procedure. The pancakes made even more of a mess, falling apart in the process. Hosea started laughing. Justice and Grace looked at him and then at DJ, and they started laughing also. At first, DJ maintained his cause without allowing for the distraction, but after a minute looked up and saw everyone laughing at him and started laughing back. They all laughed together for a few minutes before they were able to focus back on their food and start eating again. The kids had all started eating before Hosea cut into his pancake and raised the fork to his mouth, but before he could bite it, the doorbell rang.

The church bell gongs echoed through the house, and Hosea glanced in the direction of the distant front door. Justice and Grace looked at Dad and each other in wonder as they chewed.

They didn't hear the doorbell often. People didn't come to the house unannounced, so when they came through the car gate, someone in the house would already be coming to greet them long before they could get to the door. So, hearing the doorbell was both strange and startling; it was almost like an alarm going off.

Hosea looked around at the kids and thought for a moment about who it could be. Grace shrugged her shoulders, and Justice followed her lead, gesturing his fork and knife in the air. "Stay here," Hosea said as he put down his fork and pushed his chair back away from the table. He passed through three rooms before he got to the front entry. He looked at the monitors near the door and saw a woman in blue jeans and a well-worn Hawaiian shirt with her head drooped and long blond hair hiding her face. *Could it be?* His mouth fell open as he gawked at the figure on the monitors. The lone figure stood still.

A chill rushed through his body and left him shivering. He moved toward the door and reached out to open it but paused to look at his trembling hand. He unlocked the door and pulled the handle toward him to reveal the woman on his front step. He heard her quiet sobs and could see tears falling. After a few seconds, she lifted a hand and parted her hair just enough to see as she slowly looked up at him. Her eyes were bloodshot and swollen; her nose was red and running. With quivering lips and a faltering voice, she whispered, "Will you forgive me?"

His eyes widened, but he couldn't move. He stood there staring at her. Waves of hurt and pain and anguish swept over him as he shook his head in disbelief, and then waves of love and compassion. She lowered her chin and closed her eyes in shame. His eyes welled with tears, and he stepped forward and embraced her limp body, and they rocked back and forth sobbing. She lifted her hands to hug him back as they swayed. They both continued sobbing and rocking and turning until Grace and Justice appeared at the door.

They both froze for a moment at the door, gawking, until Grace cried out, "Mommy?" and rushed to embrace them both and Justice came in behind her on their other side. After another moment, DJ came and joined in, smearing syrup everywhere he touched. They swayed and spun, and eventually, they all lost balance and dumped together onto the lawn. Then they all started laughing. The kids scurried up so all their foreheads were together, laughing and crying, lying in a heap together on the ground. Candace found DJ's sticky hands and licked them for a moment, and again, they all burst into laughter.

The end.

ABOUT AUTHOR

Joseph Descans was born on June 24, 1964, to Gene and Verna Descans in Indianapolis, Indiana. His parents divorced, and at age seven and Joseph moved to San Diego, California, with his mother and younger sister, Debbie. Joseph graduated from Torrey Pines High School in 1982 and from Point Loma Nazarene University in 2000 with a BA in literature. He is a single dad with four children, two cats, and three chickens and still lives in San Diego. He is a freelance writer, editor, writing coach, contractor, certified arborist, cat-stuck-in-a-tree rescuer, and former professional surfer. His favorite pastimes are surfing, snowboarding, and fishing with his four children—Lily, Giuseppe, Abraham, and Hezekiah—and friends.

Please email all book content questions and comments to the author at: HoseaAuthor@AOL.com.

CPSIA information can be obtained
at www.ICGtesting.com
Printed in the USA
BVHW090313300922
648337BV00005B/18